"The story is great . . . [Brock Cole] has talent with a capital *T*."　　—*Los Angeles Times Book Review*

"Back in the real world, grown-ups control their lives. But now, suddenly, the boy and girl feel powerful . . . *The Goats* contains some secrets about being 13."　　—*The Washington Post Book World*

"A beautifully written and persuasive first novel."
　　—*The New York Times Book Review*

"One of the finest books for teenagers to appear in a long time."　　—*Philadelphia Inquirer*

An ALA Best Book for Young Adults

An ALA Notable Book

A New York Times Book Review Notable Book

A School Library Journal Best Book of the Year

A Booklist Children's Editors' Choice

ALSO BY BROCK COLE
Celine

THE GOATS

BROCK COLE

aerial fiction
Farrar, Straus and Giroux

FOR SUSAN

CONTENTS

THE GOATS

The Island

WHEN HE came back to the beach with wood for the fire Bryce grabbed him from behind. The firewood scattered, bouncing off his knees and shins.

"Okay, Bryce," he said. "Cut it out." He tried to sound unafraid, even a little bored.

Bryce pulled his elbows back until they were almost touching. The boy tried to look up at the other kids. They turned their faces away, squinting out over the lake or frowning up into the trees above the beach.

"Hey," Bryce said. "Do I have to do everything?"

For a moment no one moved, and then Murphy shrugged and knelt down heavily in front of the boy. He was frowning, as if he had to do something disagreeable.

"Don't," said the boy.

Murphy pulled down his shorts. The boy's knees folded, and as he fell Bryce tugged his sweat shirt over his head. It was a new shirt. It had the camp emblem of the Tall Pine on the front. Someone sat on his knees so they could pull off his shoes and socks. Then they let him go. He scuttled sideways on his hands and knees into a thicket of reeds and fell on his side. He could hardly breathe.

"Come on, Howie," Murphy said. "You're a goat. Don't you get it?"

The boy curled up tightly, squeezing his eyes shut, waiting for the world to explode.

"I don't think he gets it," Murphy said.

The boy didn't move. He heard the canoes being shoved back into the water. There was a clatter of paddles and a loud splash. Someone laughed.

"Do you think he's okay?" Murphy whispered. No one answered.

When he was sure they were gone, the boy sat up. He was stiff, and his arms ached. His glasses had been knocked askew. He took them off, straightened one of the bows, and put them on again. His hands were shaking.

It was beginning to get dark. He couldn't see the canoes. Across the lake someone had turned on the lights at the camp boathouse. He could see the masts of the class boats swaying above the dock. They looked very far away.

"Damn," he said softly.

He didn't know what he was supposed to do now. Nobody had said. He didn't understand why they had taken his clothes and left him alone on the island. He thought that someone else would probably know what to do, but he didn't. It was because he was so out of it.

The mosquitoes were starting to bite. He had some repellent on his face and legs, but not all over. If he had known what they were planning, he would have hidden a bottle somewhere when he went to find firewood.

Slowly he got to his feet, brushing off the sand and pine needles clinging to his skin. He had never been naked outside before, and the feeling of being completely exposed was worse standing up. He wanted to crouch down again in the reeds, but he forced himself to move. There had to be something he could do.

It was a relief to find a path which led up toward the center of the island. In the shelter of the trees he felt less vulnerable. He wished it was pitch dark. He had never been afraid of the dark.

At the top of the island was an old tent platform. It had a canvas roof and sides of wood and screening. He stood at the edge of the clearing and looked at the tent platform and listened, but he couldn't hear anything except leaves rubbing against one another and the little slapping noises the waves made on the shore below. He crossed the clearing quickly and fumbled with the latch of the screen door. He was suddenly anxious to have the four walls around him.

He wasn't ready when someone inside said, "Go away."

His legs bounced him across the clearing before he could stop them, but there was nowhere to go. There was absolutely nowhere to go. He took a deep breath and walked quietly back to the door. He sat down on the steps, keeping his front hidden. He could hear someone crying inside. It sounded like a girl. She was gulping and crying at the same time.

"Hey," he said.

"I said go away."

"Hey, I can't. They took my clothes."

He waited, but there was no response.

"The mosquitoes are killing me. They really are."

Again there was no answer, but he heard a brief scuffling inside, and then the catch being released. As he pushed open the door, something black and shapeless scuttled into a corner. He didn't know what to do. He was glad it was dark inside.

"Did they leave anything?" he asked finally.

"There're some sandwiches and stuff on the table."

"I mean some blankets or clothes. I'm freezing."

"There's just one blanket."

And *she* had that, he thought. He felt his way to the table in the center of the room and ran his hand lightly over the surface. There was a package done up in plastic wrap, a box of matches, and something that felt like a candle lantern.

He left the table and groped his way toward a corner as far from the girl as possible. He found a cot there with a bare, damp mattress and a heavy pillow smelling of mildew. He sat down on the cot, holding the pillow on his lap.

"What are we going to do?" he asked.

"Nothing. Sit here."

"They'll probably come back in the morning."

"I know it."

He wondered what that would be like. Would they sneak up and try to peek through the screens, or would they be yelling and dancing around? He didn't know what went on in their heads. Sometimes he thought he knew, but then it turned out that he didn't.

"Hey. There's a candle lantern. I'm going to light it."

"Don't."

"I'm freezing, I tell you."

Holding the pillow to his front, he felt his way back to the table. By leaning against it he could keep the pillow in place while he lit the candle in the lantern.

She was huddled on the floor, completely wrapped up in a ratty old army blanket. Her face was turned away, so he couldn't see it. Her hair was stringy and damp-looking. He wondered if she was naked under the blanket. Probably she was. That would be the joke, wouldn't it? Bryce must think they would jump all over each other if they didn't have any clothes on.

He held his hands over the lantern. They burned but didn't seem to get warm. On the table beside the sandwiches was a deck of playing cards. They were the dirty ones that Arnold Metcalf showed around to his friends. The boy had never seen them up close. He hadn't wanted anyone to know he was interested. Now he didn't want to look at them. The top card had a picture of a man and a woman crumpled together. It had nothing to do with him. It was about as interesting as a picture of a dentist drilling a tooth.

Bryce must be crazy. Arnold Metcalf and Murphy—they were all crazy. Trying to guess what went on in their crazy heads was wearing him out. He retreated to the bed and sat down again, still holding the pillow over his front.

"We're the goats, I guess," he said, hoping she could explain what was happening to them.

"So?"

"So nothing."

She still wouldn't look at him, but he could see who it was now. He couldn't remember her name. She was one of the real dogs. Bryce had classified all the girls into queens, princesses, dogs, and real dogs. Bryce should never have called her a real dog. He should never have called anyone a dog, because it made you think he looked like a dog himself. A big pink bulldog. Still, she shouldn't wear big designer glasses if her eyes were so bad. If you had thick glasses, they became thicker and thicker the bigger they were. His ophthalmologist had told him that.

He was beginning to feel hungry. He wondered if it would be safe to eat the sandwiches, but he decided not to. They might have put dope or something like that in them.

"I thought this was supposed to be a cookout," he said, trying to laugh. "We brought hot dogs and stuff." He remembered telling the others that they didn't have enough hot dogs. He had even argued about it, as if he was the only one who could count. Bryce had agreed and said that they were lucky he was such a brain. What a fool he had been.

"What did they tell you?" he asked.

She reached out a skinny brown arm and picked at a piece of rotten screen over her head.

"They told me Julie Christiansen was going to be the goat. We were all supposed to come out and go skinny-dipping, and then we were going to lose her."

He didn't know what to say. She was an even bigger jerk than he was, thinking that Julie Christiansen could ever be a goat. He wondered why she would tell a story that made her look so dumb.

"I thought they liked me," she said, and started to cry again.

"Hey," he said.

"Shut up."

He shut up. He was beginning to feel really cold. His jaw shuddered, and he felt goose bumps break out on his arms. He studied the top of her head in the dim light from the lantern, trying to guess what kind of person she was.

"I'm really cold," he said. "Do you want to split the blanket? Maybe we could find something to cut it with."

She looked at him for the first time. Her glasses made her eyes look little and close together. He could tell she hated him, so he looked away.

There was a fireplace at one end of the tent platform. There wasn't any wood, but he could gather some sticks and pinecones outside. He could build a fire. He could use Arnold's dirty playing cards to start it, but he didn't know how he'd hold on to the pillow at the same time.

"How are you going to act tomorrow?" he asked after a while.

She shrugged, pulling down a big piece of the screen. He wished she wouldn't do that. There were enough mosquitoes inside, anyway.

"I mean, do you think we should act like we thought it was a joke, or what?"

She started crying again. It was awful to have to sit there and watch her cry.

"What . . ." he said carefully, trying to think of something that would quiet her down. "What if we weren't here when they came back?"

"What do you mean? Where'd we go?"

"What if we swam over to the shore? We could sneak back to camp and get some clothes, and then just act like nothing had happened."

"That's nuts. It's miles to shore."

"No, it isn't. I bet I could swim that far." He was beginning to feel enthusiastic about his plan, although he didn't believe himself that they could do it. It was good to think about, though. He could see those jerks when he walked into breakfast, acting as if nothing had happened at all. They would want to know how he'd gotten back, but they wouldn't be able to ask, and he would just say something witty about the eggs. He'd say, "Hey! This is the same egg I got yesterday." Something like that.

"It's a dumb idea, and anyway, I can't swim very well."

"Come on. There's a big log down on the shore. I saw it when I was getting wood for the cookout. We could shove it in and paddle over."

"No, I said. I don't want to talk about it anymore." Her nose was running, and there wasn't anything for her to wipe it with but her fingers.

"Well," he said, "I'm going to build a fire. Do you want to help?"

She pulled the blanket back up over her head. He could freeze to death and she wouldn't care. He sidled over to the door, keeping the pillow over his front in case she tried to look.

Outside, it was very dark now. He could hear the mosquitoes drifting around his head. Their feathery wings brushed against his bare skin. He dropped his pillow on the steps and tried to work fast, dodging the insects and feeling for pinecones with his toes. He couldn't hold very many at a time. He'd have to make about a million trips unless he found something bigger.

When he heard the noise he dropped everything he had picked up and listened. He didn't hear it again, but he knew what it was. The sound of a paddle knocking against the gunwale of a canoe. He took a couple of steps toward the tent platform, and then turned and hustled back down the path until he could see over the lake toward the camp.

The moon was just showing, getting ready to set, but there was enough light to turn the lake silver. He could make out one, no two, dark shapes coming toward the island. They were still some distance away.

She looked up, startled, when he pushed open the door. He realized that he'd forgotten to find his pillow, and so he covered himself with both hands.

"Listen. They're coming back."

"What?"

"They're coming back. Some of them, anyway."

"Oh, God, Oh, God . . ." She pulled the blanket over her head and started crying again.

"Stop it, will you? They'll hear!"

"I don't care," she said in a muffled voice, but she quieted down.

"Come on, then. We've got to get out of here."

"What do you mean?"

"What do you mean, what do I mean? Do you want to be here when they come?"

She thought about it. "They wouldn't hurt us or anything, would they? They'll probably just sneak up or something."

He couldn't believe that she was so feeble.

"What's the matter with you? Do you want them spying on us?"

She shook her head, her rubbery face going all out of shape again.

"Well, then, listen. We'll go down to the shore, and when they come sneaking up, we'll grab their canoes. We'll leave them here. They'll be the goats, don't you get it?"

It seemed to sink in finally.

"What'll we do?" she asked, trying to get up without letting the blanket open.

"Just come on and be quiet."

"Shall we put out the candle?"

"No," he said after a moment's thought. "They'll come up slow if they see the light. It'll give us more time."

Once outside, he forgot about keeping himself covered up. It was dark and not important anymore. It was the others he cared about. They weren't going to see him if he could help it. He grabbed a corner of her blanket and led the way down the path. She held on as if he was trying to take it away from her.

Near the shore they pushed through some brush until they found a place to hide in a clump of black alder at the water's edge. They were a safe distance from the little beach. He decided it would be easier to wade over to the canoes than try to push their way back through the bushes, so he pulled her down close to the water.

The canoes were near the shore now. He could see that there were only four people. He didn't like that. It seemed more menacing, as if something was planned which had to be kept secret, even from the others who had left him on the island. He began to feel weak inside.

The girl was snuffling beside him.

"Be quiet," he whispered.

"It's the mosquitoes. They're in my mouth, everything."

"I said be quiet." He fumbled in the blanket until he found her hand and squeezed it hard. He wanted to believe he could hurt someone if he had to.

The people in the canoes beached them without a sound. It was too dark to see who they were, but they were big. They huddled together for a moment, whispering, and then two of them broke away and disappeared up the path.

The others stayed by the canoes. One of them lit a cigarette, and the other picked something up from the beach and flicked it out over the water. The boy heard a soft *plunk! plunk! plunk!* The person was skipping stones.

The boy waited, but he didn't know what he was waiting for anymore. His beautiful plan was coming apart like wet paper. He and the girl could never get the canoes away from the guards on the beach.

His brain seemed to have stopped working. He didn't know what he was going to do. He had never been so cold in his life. He wondered what was going to happen to them.

"There're some people still there," the girl whispered. "What do we do now?" She didn't sound sarcastic. She wanted to know. The cold seemed to solidify into a hard little lump somewhere deep inside him.

"Come on," he whispered, putting his lips close to

her ear. "We've got to get away. We're going down into the water."

"But I can't swim, I told you."

"You won't have to. There's that log I told you about. I'll push you."

The water felt warm, warmer than the air. It made him feel better. He moved quietly, not making any splashes. When he was a few feet out, crouching so that only his head showed, he looked back to see if she was coming.

She came down into the water still wrapped in her blanket, and then let it drift away.

It didn't take long for them to work their way along the shore until the canoes were out of sight. The girl was clutching at him, afraid of the water. He could feel it in her stiff fingers digging into his shoulder.

They found the log just as the moon was setting. There was nothing but starlight now to show the shape of the distant shore. It looked black and lumpy, like a pile of coal.

He dragged the log into the water, trying to be as quiet as he could. It floated awfully low. He wondered if it could actually support them. Overhead, the beam of a flashlight flickered amid the treetops and was gone.

"Come on, now. Don't try to ride it. Just hold on."

He transferred her grasping hands to the wood. She was making too much noise, gasping and trying to hold her head high out of the water.

"Relax," he said. "Just try to kind of float along. Just keep your mouth out of the water."

"I'm afraid. Maybe you'd better go without me."

"No," he said. He didn't try to explain. He knew he was afraid to leave her alone, but even more important, it wouldn't be good enough. He wanted them both to disappear. To disappear completely.

Very quietly, hardly daring to breathe, he walked the log out into the water until the muddy bottom dropped away and there was nothing there at all.

Margo Cutter, senior counselor, came down to the beach still carrying the bag of clothes. Max didn't shine his flashlight in her face, of course, but he could tell by her voice that it must be grim.

"They're not there," she said.

Max flipped his cigarette into the water. "Well, they must be somewhere around. They wouldn't try to swim for it, would they?"

"I don't think so. Laura can't swim. She's afraid of the water. What about Howie?"

Max shrugged. "I don't know. He can swim all right, but it's a mile and a half, and he's kind of wimpy."

He knew at once that he shouldn't have said that, because it annoyed Margo and set her off again. "I just don't understand how anybody could have thought that this would be even remotely funny."

"Yeah," Max said, trying to sound conciliatory. "We'd better see if we can find them. We should have brought some dope for the mosquitoes. They're pretty bad."

"I mean it. I don't know what I'm going to say to her. She told me she wanted to go home, and I told her that this was such a wonderful place and that she'd make such wonderful friends. Some friends. I tell you, Max, I'm ready to quit over this. I never want to see some of those smug little brats again."

"Come on, Margo. It's not that serious. I know it was a dumb stunt, but they didn't mean anything—you know—harmful."

Margo shone her flashlight right in his face. "No? Well, what the hell did they mean? You tell me, Max. I really want to know. What the hell did they mean?"

The Cottage

WHEN THEY were close enough to the shore to touch bottom, she couldn't walk. She tried to, but she kept falling over. Finally he had to drag her out of the water, holding her by the armpits. He dragged her over a narrow muddy beach and up on some grass before his feet slipped out from under him and he sat down with a bump.

He sat there panting while she lay between his legs, staring up at the sky through glasses pebbled with water. It was beginning to get light, with that pale dawn light that robs everything of color.

He looked at her body. It was long and white. She had no breasts, just two shriveled nipples. At the bottom of her belly was a little patch of hair, like a Hitler mustache. That meant that she was more mature than he was. He didn't have any hair yet. The other boys called him Baldy. It was supposed to be funny, because he had thick curly hair on his head.

We're just little kids, he thought, and felt waves of self-pity sweep over him. He cried for a few minutes, and then stopped. She was shuddering and breathing funny, and her skin was cold, like damp rubber.

"Get up," he said.

She didn't say anything. Her eyes were open, but she didn't say anything.

The grass they were sitting on was short. His brain had to work on that fact for a moment before he realized that it had been cut. They were sitting on somebody's lawn. He looked around and saw a dark house tilting over them.

"Get up," he said again. "There's a house. We'll get some help."

She rolled slowly off his legs and curled up in a ball on her side, sagging into the grass.

He stared at her stupidly for a minute, and then got to his feet and climbed the lawn to the house. It was small and empty. A summer cottage. Large board shutters had been fastened over the windows. Behind it was a grove of dark trees. He could hear the drum of tires as someone drove by on a hidden highway. There was nothing else.

She hadn't moved when he got back to her.

"Nobody's there," he said. "It's shut up. There's a

road somewhere. Do you think you can walk? We've got to get some help."

"You go," she said quietly, into the grass. "You get someone."

He didn't know if he could. He was shaking with cold, and he wondered if they were going to die. It seemed ridiculous, to die on the front lawn of someone's summer cottage. There was a road not far away. At camp everyone would be snoring in their sleeping bags and soon they would be eating breakfast. It was summer. How could they be dying like this?

"I'm going to try to break in," he said.

The door was locked and the shutters over the windows were fastened with big rusty wing nuts. When he tried to turn them, blood came out from under his fingernails. His skin was white and shriveled. He thought he would show the people who owned the house his fingers. Then maybe they would understand why it had been important that he break in. As he looked at his hands, he became angry at the people because they had locked up their house and because they weren't there to help. He found a stone and smashed at the wing nuts on one of the window shutters until they broke off and the shutter fell onto the porch with an enormous crash. Shocked, he waited, afraid that someone might hear. It occurred to him that he wasn't thinking very clearly.

The window wasn't locked. He lifted the sash and looked inside. The cottage was small, no more than a single room. There was a sink and some cupboards on one side, a table in the center, and a bed. Light fell in pale bars through the cracks in the shutters. He could just make out some blankets and a tattered quilt folded on the bed.

He went back to the beach and made the girl stand up. She could walk if he helped her, but her knees didn't seem to work properly. They kept locking with every step.

When he got her through the window, he made her lie down on the bed and tried to cover them both with the blankets. It was hard to do. He had trouble getting the blankets unfolded, and they grated like Brillo against his bare legs. When he had done the best he could, he lay back. He didn't feel any warmer. His hands hurt and his teeth were chattering. She began to curl up again, burrowing against him like an animal, thrusting her face into his neck and digging her fists into his ribs.

"Hey," he said, "what's the matter with you?" She didn't hear him. He wondered if she was feeling warm inside. He knew that when you froze to death you were supposed to feel warm inside just before the end.

He took off his glasses and folded them neatly, but there was no place to put them. He looked up at the ceiling. Someone had pinned a centerfold directly overhead. It was of a lady with her legs spread. She looked as if she were falling on him from an enormous distance. It was such a joke. It was such a joke he wanted to laugh.

. . .

He woke up when she rolled away from him. He could see blue sky out of the window. His hands hurt, but he was warm. Deliciously warm.

"Are you okay?" he asked.

She squinted at him with bleary distaste, as if she had stepped in something disagreeable and wasn't sure what it was. Her glasses were all cockeyed, but still on her nose.

"Where are we?" she said finally.

"In the house. The cottage. I broke in."

"You broke in?" She stared at him. "You just broke in? They could put us in jail!"

"No, they couldn't," he said, but he wasn't really sure. "You were passing out all over the place. I had to."

She grimaced and wiped her hands against her chest as if they had dirt on them.

"I feel sick." She craned her neck around. "Aren't there any clothes or something?"

"I don't know. Shall I look around?" He waited until she turned away, and then he got out of bed slowly. It hurt to stand up. His legs and arms ached. He pulled out the drawers in a cupboard by the sink and found some towels, a pair of pants stiff with paint, a grubby sweat shirt, and a couple of T-shirts.

He put on the pants. He couldn't stand on one leg, so he had to sit down in a chair to do it. Then he put on one of the T-shirts. The clothes were too big. They were for an adult.

"This is all there is," he said, taking the girl the sweat shirt.

"That's okay. Give me that other undershirt, too."

She drew the sweat shirt up over her arms and lay back, looking at the ceiling where the centerfold was floating like some kind of angel gone bad. The boy went back to the sink and rummaged in the shelves overhead. There were cans of fruit cocktail and chicken noodle soup and an open box of saltines. In a rusty refrigerator he found a half-empty bottle of ginger ale. He carried the crackers and the ginger ale back to the bed.

"Eat some," he said.

The crackers were soft and stuck to the roof of his mouth. She couldn't swallow the crackers, but she drank some of the ginger ale. It was warm and flat. Then she dozed off again.

He lay down carefully beside her, propped up on one elbow so he could look at her face. Her hair was matted and her forehead puffy with mosquito blotches. Her ears were waxy and not very clean. They had been pierced, but she didn't have earrings.

He couldn't remember now why she was supposed to be a real dog. He couldn't even tell whether she was pretty or not. She had long eyelashes and her lips curled up at the corners. That seemed very remarkable to him.

When he woke up the second time, the girl was trying to crawl over him.

"What's the matter?"

"I'm going to be sick. I have to go to the bathroom."

"There isn't one."

"What?" She crouched over him, unbelieving.

"There isn't one. It must be out in back."

She looked around, a little desperate. "Do I have to crawl out the window?"

He nodded.

"God, I don't think I can. I'm really going to be sick."

"Use the sink," he said. He was afraid she would be sick on him if she stayed where she was.

"The sink? How can I use the sink?"

"I don't know. Just do it."

She looked at him as if he were crazy, but nonetheless lurched out of bed and toward the sink. She didn't make it. He looked away, trying not to hear.

When she had finished, she stayed where she was, her mouth wide open and twisted down at the corners. She was crying, but no sound was coming out.

Reluctantly he got up and went over to her. "It's okay," he said. "Really, it's okay."

She made a horrible gulping sound. "Look at the mess!"

"It's okay. It's just ginger ale, mostly." He grabbed a dish towel that had dried into a hard, shriveled wad and tried to wipe her face. She swatted at his hand, knocking her glasses off so that they skittered across the floor.

"Oh, God, I need somebody to take care of me!" She blundered past him to the bed, crawling under the covers as if she wanted to hide there forever. He found her glasses and carried them over to the bed. They weren't broken. She wouldn't look at him, so he folded

them and put them on the mattress by her head. She
had stopped crying. She was staring at the ceiling and
sighing through clenched teeth. She kept shuddering
over and over.

After a few minutes she stopped.

"Are you okay?"

She nodded.

"You want something to eat?"

She shook her head, still staring at the ceiling.

"I could make some soup. Maybe you'd feel better
if you ate something. There's chicken noodle or chicken
noodle."

She wouldn't smile.

"What do you want?"

"Chicken noodle."

He found a can opener in a drawer and opened one
of the cans of soup. He dumped the soup into a pot,
but when he held the can under the faucet and turned
the tap nothing happened. He found a bucket behind
the curtain under the sink.

"I've got to get some water out of the lake. They
must have turned off the water here. Okay?" She didn't
say anything. She was still staring at the centerfold as
if it might swoop down and smother her.

When he climbed through the window he could see
that it was going to be a beautiful day.

He carried the bucket down to the water's edge and
looked out toward the island. They hadn't swum across
the shortest way. The island was far down the lake.

He could see the camp launch, a big white boat with

varnished top sides, sticking its nose up into the trees there. As he watched, a small gray outboard worked its way into view from behind the island. A man in a white shirt was standing in the bow looking into the water.

The boy filled the bucket and went back to the house. He splashed some of the water into the soup and put it on the stove. It was a butane camping stove and it lit without difficulty. The rest of the water he sluiced over the damp spot on the floor. He could hear it dripping through the cracks in the floorboards into the earth below.

When the soup was hot he found two cracked cereal bowls and poured the soup carefully into them. There were some spoons in the drawer where he had found the can opener. He put a spoon into each of the bowls and carried them over to the bed.

The girl had torn up the second T-shirt and fashioned it into a pair of panties. They looked like a cross between a diaper and a bikini. She put them on under the covers.

"We should keep track of the stuff we use," he said. "So we can pay them back."

"It was an old shirt," she said, as if he had meant to criticize her.

"Yeah, I know. That's okay."

When the soup was gone, he opened a can of fruit cocktail. She poured it into their empty bowls, dividing up the red cherries evenly without comment.

"I don't think we should stay here," he said when they had finished.

"Why? What's wrong? Do you think the people might come back?"

"I saw the launch out by the island when I went to get the water. They must be looking for us. They'll probably figure out that we came over here."

The girl dropped her spoon and picked at a knot in the old quilt.

"Where can we go?" she said finally.

The boy shrugged. He had an idea, a picture really, of them camping out in the pine woods around the lake. Nobody knew where they were, but they were there, living like Indians.

It was not something he wanted her to consider. He knew she would just tell him how crazy it was.

"I wish we could just disappear," he said finally. The girl was watching him. "They could look for us and couldn't find us. They'd be wondering what happened, but they would never know."

The girl stared at the quilt again, looking into his vision, or maybe one of her own.

"Yeah," she said. "That would be neat."

He could hear a car somewhere, honking its horn, and a dog barking.

"I think I'd better call my mom," she said after a moment. That made him feel bad. He didn't know why. "I mean, she'll think I'm dead or something."

He nodded, not wanting to say anything.

"Do you want to call your mom or dad?" she asked. "Are they still married?"

"Yeah. They're in Turkey somewhere. I've got the address, but I left it back at camp."

"What are they doing there?"

"They're archaeologists. They're working. Excavating some stuff."

"That sounds interesting. Did you ever, you know, go and help them?"

"No. I went a couple of times when I was little. It was kind of boring, really." He thought of the flat dusty site. The fragments of pottery laid out on the wooden tables with the white canvas awnings flapping overhead. Everything was covered with a reddish-gold dust. Small brown falcons with sharp pointed wings flew overhead.

"I liked Greece better, but they don't go there anymore. They thought I'd be better off here, where I could make some friends my age."

"Yeah. My mom thought that, too."

The flat bars of light shining through the cracks in the shutter had turned to gold as the sun rose. It was odd, but even though the light was brighter it was harder to see.

"Listen," she said. "What if I call my mom and tell her to come and get us? Both of us, I mean. You could stay with my mom and me until your parents got back."

"You really think so? That would be neat. You sure she wouldn't mind?"

"I don't know. I don't think so. She's always after me to invite kids from school over." She paused. "I'm socially retarded for my age," she said with a certain dignity.

"Yeah. Me too." They looked at each other silently.

"Well, let's try it. We could have a great time, going to movies and stuff. The Museum of Science and Industry is just a couple of blocks away. They have all sorts of interesting exhibits and things."

"Yeah? I think I'd like to do that."

"They've got a big heart you can walk into, and these people all sliced up in thin little slices. They're stuck in these glass doors, and on the first door is just, I don't know, an elbow or something, but then you turn the doors and you can see everything. All their insides."

He stared at her. "Are they real people? I mean, really real?"

"Yeah. There's a man and a lady. All sliced up."

"But where would they get them? Who would they get to cut up like that?"

The girl shrugged. "I don't know. Maybe the people didn't have any family."

They sat quietly for a moment, thinking about the sliced-up man and woman.

"Well," said the boy. "There're some phones down at the municipal beach. Maybe you could call from there. Maybe we wouldn't have to go back to camp at all."

"God, that would be great." She wiped her hands

on the quilt. "I've got to get cleaned up," she said. "I'm such a mess."

She got out of bed, still a little shaky, but he could tell she felt better.

They crawled out the window and went down to the lake together. The girl tucked her sweat shirt up around her waist and waded into the water, scrubbing her arms and legs. The boy looked around carefully before he squatted down to wash his face. There was no one near. A man was fishing from a rickety dock several hundred feet down the shore, and the launch was still moored out by the island. The small gray boat was gone.

"Do I look okay?" said the girl, coming out of the water.

He regarded her thoughtfully. "Yeah, I guess so. You look like you might have a swimsuit on under your shirt. You shouldn't have gotten it wet, though. You can see through it."

She pulled up the hem of the sweat shirt and looked at her stomach calmly.

"It'll dry by the time we get to the beach." She wrinkled her nose at him critically. "Those pants look kind of queer."

"Yeah, but there wasn't anything else."

"Let's cut them off. Maybe they won't look so peculiar then."

They found a serrated knife among the kitchen utensils, and the girl hacked off the legs of the pants while he watched, wrapped in the quilt.

"We should really pay for all this stuff," he said uneasily. "I mean the pants and the shirts."

"And the soup. We'll come back later and explain. They probably won't mind."

When he put on the pants he tied two keepers together with a bit of string and pulled the T-shirt down over the bunched-up waistband.

"Well," she said, "they still look a little strange, but probably nobody will say anything." She was trying to brush out her hair with a vegetable brush that she had found hanging over the sink. "Be careful when you sit down, though."

"Why?"

"Well, you can see."

They folded up the blankets and quilt and washed the pot and dishes in the lake. The boy found a garbage can behind the cottage near the outhouse and put the bottle, the empty saltine carton, and the tin cans inside. As they left, the girl helped him prop the shutter back up on the window. They couldn't fasten it because he had pounded most of the wing nuts off, but he didn't think that someone just passing by would notice.

Behind the cottage was a dirt road. They followed it toward the highway, where they could hear cars passing.

"How far is it to the beach?" she asked.

"I don't know. Do you think we should try to hitch a ride?"

"I'm not supposed to hitchhike. It's dangerous."

"Yeah. They might be looking for us, anyway."

"We should probably stay off the highway, then."

"Okay. We'll just try to stay close to the shore."

It was not difficult. The lakefront was heavily built up, and between the cottages and the highway was a network of driveways and dirt roads. It took longer to walk along these than along the highway, but it was easy on their bare feet, and they didn't seem to attract any attention. They might be just two kids staying at someone else's cottage.

A crowd of local teenagers was swimming around the public boat launch. The boys wore cutoff jeans instead of swimsuits. They had white, hard bellies and dark-brown arms. They threw themselves into the water recklessly, each trying to make a bigger splash than the others. Two girls in bikinis smoked cigarettes and watched. Their faces were expressionless. No one would know if they were impressed.

The boy and the girl circled the crowd warily, walking behind a rusty Cadillac convertible and a pickup with a roll bar in the back.

"Wait a minute," said the girl. As he watched she walked over to the door of the pickup and looked inside. The window must have been rolled down, because she suddenly stepped up on the running board and reached inside. She came back, her face stiff and expressionless, one hand clenched in a fist at her side.

"Keep walking," she said.

"What did you do?" he asked, feeling panicky.

She opened her fist for a second without stopping. He saw a glint of silver.

"Hey, that's stealing! You should put it back!"

She stopped and looked at him blankly. "You put it back," she said. She thrust the change into his hand and stalked off, holding her elbows.

He knew he wasn't going to put the money back. When he caught up with her he tried to look at her face, but she kept her head down.

"Hey," he said, "I'm sorry. I must be a drain brain."

She turned on him angrily. "We need it, don't we? I mean, how am I supposed to call my mom? They didn't leave us anything. They took our clothes and everything."

"It's okay. I was just being stupid. Okay?"

"Okay."

"Okay, then."

After a minute she said, "How much is it?"

He looked at the change in his hand. "A dollar forty. How did you know it was there?"

"I didn't. I just remembered that people sometimes keep change in those little compartments on their dashboards. For tolls and stuff. They probably won't even miss it. We could pay them back, anyway."

She was starting to limp. She must have hurt her foot on one of the roots that ran through the dust in the road.

"Yes," he said. "We'll pay them back. We'll pay them back for everything."

The Municipal Beach

IT WAS too early for the municipal beach to be crowded. A few mothers with aluminum folding chairs sat on the strip of yellow sand that the township had dumped over the dark clay beach. Their feet were mired in shopping bags full of towels, yarn, and toys. Some small children squatted in the shallows, and a young couple was spreading a beach towel which looked like a giant dollar bill a few yards away.

Above the concession stand with its Pepsi-Cola sign hovered a blue haze from the grill. Behind the stand were two rows of wooden cubicles where people could change their clothes. The public telephones stood in their plastic bubbles next to the path leading to the parking lot.

"Do I look okay?" the girl asked again, pulling at the bottom of her sweat shirt.

"Sure you look okay. You look great."

She made a face so he wouldn't think she believed him, and they came down out of the trees and started to cross the bumpy lawn to the telephones. They had to watch their step because of the little metal tabs torn from the tops of beer and soft-drink cans that glittered in the grass.

The boy sat down on one of the railroad ties that held back the gravel of the parking lot. He put his hands under his legs to keep his pants closed, and watched the girl as she pushed a quarter into a telephone.

Mrs. Pritzer stuck her head into Maddy Golden's office.

"It's Laura." She kept her face carefully blank, to show that it wasn't her place to express an opinion. "Line 5."

What now, Maddy asked herself, reaching for the phone on her desk. Mrs. Pritzer was still standing in the open doorway. Maddy looked at her, raising her eyebrows in inquiry.

"It was a collect call, Mrs. Golden. I hope I was right to accept the charges. I thought it might be important, even if it is a personal call."

"Yes. Yes, it's all right, Mrs. Pritzer."

The older woman withdrew, some obscure accounting of her own satisfied.

"Hello, Laura? Honey? Everything okay?"

"Yeah." There was a long pause. "Mom?"

Maddy tried to keep her voice bright, confiding. "Yes? What is it, honey? You know you shouldn't call me at the office unless it is really important. I mean an emergency or something."

"Yeah, Mom. Mom? I've got to come home."

Why? Why couldn't Laura adjust to camp? Why did her life have to be so tangled, so difficult? The questions remained unasked, clenched down in Maddy's throat.

"Listen, Laura," she said carefully, "we talked about this before, and we decided we'd give it another chance. Do you remember? I thought you'd made some friends. You did tell me that, you know."

"I know, but you've got to come get me, Mom."

"Don't start crying! You're not a baby anymore! Now tell me what's wrong. Can you do that? Are you having trouble with the other kids?"

"Yeah."

"Well? What kind of trouble?"

There was another long pause.

"I don't know. They're all really despicable. They're all hypocrites."

Maddy sighed. Laura's favorite words. What had she done to raise a child so stiff and unbending? She was a little prude, that was part of the problem. No wonder the other kids gave her a rough time.

"Listen, Laura, I don't think that's a real reason. I

mean, I know that some people aren't very nice, but you have to learn to deal with them, not just at camp, but everywhere. I mean, I have to deal with people who aren't very nice, too, you know."

"I've got to come home, Mom. Now." She was wailing. Literally wailing. Maddy wondered if Mrs. Pritzer was listening on the extension, twisting things around in that dried-up brain of hers.

"Laura. You are not listening."

"It's really important, Mom!"

"Okay, okay." Maddy put her hand over the receiver and sat back, closing her eyes, trying to stay calm.

"Okay," she began again. "There's a Parents' Weekend coming up, isn't there?"

"Saturday. But you said you weren't coming."

"Well, I am coming. I mean, if you're having problems, I've got to, haven't I? We'll talk about it then. Okay?"

"I don't know, Mom. I really . . ."

"Laura, I don't know what else I can do. I'm trying to earn a living. For both of us. You can really help me if you try to manage things by yourself for a change. Talk to Miss Cutter if you want. You said she was very nice, didn't you?"

"She's okay, but . . ."

"But nothing. This is very important, Laura. It's just two days. I really want you to show me that you can handle these problems by yourself, at least for two days. Okay?"

There was silence.

"I said okay, Laura?"

"Okay, Mom."

"All right, then. I'll see you Saturday about lunchtime. Now I want you to have a good time. Try to do something different. Are you having your period?"

The question had popped out before she could stop it. She could hear in it the fond, prying note that she had so hated in her own mother's voice.

"No." Laura swallowed the word, shutting Maddy away.

"I'm sorry, honey, I know you don't like to talk about it, but sometimes when a girl gets her period, she feels depressed. It's just a fact of life."

There was another silence and then the receiver buzzed in her ear. Laura hadn't even said goodbye. Didn't she realize how upsetting that was? Maddy had always had this dread of not saying goodbye properly. Of course Laura knew it. She was very good at picking out little ways to punish her mother.

Mrs. Pritzer stuck her head in the door again. She didn't like to use the intercom. She liked to be able to see Maddy's face if she thought the call might be interesting.

"It's a Mr. Wells."

"Who is he? What does he want?"

"He's the director. At Laura's camp," said Mrs. Pritzer. She beamed in bland triumph. "Line 3."

"Thank you, Mrs. Pritzer."

I could kill her, thought Maddy, hardly knowing

whom she meant. I could really kill her. She pushed the button on the phone angrily.

"She can't come," the girl said. "Not until Saturday."

He wasn't surprised. He had seen her crying. Her cheeks were still wet with tears. She had let them run down into the corners of her mouth.

"Saturday," he said. "What are we supposed to do until Saturday?"

"I don't know. Go back to camp, I guess."

The boy looked down to the beach, where some children were running back and forth over the sand. The sun was high enough so that the glare hurt his eyes.

"I really really don't want to do that," he said.

"Me neither. I don't know what else to do."

"Did you tell her? About us being the goats?"

The girl shook her head. She sat up and straightened her shoulders. "My mother and I don't communicate very well," she said.

The boy nodded. They watched a man with a little girl and boy trying to set up a volleyball net. The little girl was waving one of the poles around, like a flagpole without a flag.

"Don't do that, Tracy," the man said. He made his voice sound very patient, warning his daughter that in a minute he was going to get mad.

"How much money have we got left?" asked the boy. "I'm starving."

"Still a dollar forty. The operator gave me my quarter back because it was a collect call."

"Let's get a hot dog or something." They got up and walked toward the concession stand, trying to look casual.

The man behind the counter was big, with damp pink hands.

"What do you want?" he said.

There was a chalkboard propped up over the grill listing what the man sold and how much it was. The boy studied it carefully. Hot dogs were seventy-five cents. They didn't have enough for two. They could buy a hot dog and a Coke or a Mars bar.

"I don't know. You want to split a hot dog and a Coke?" he asked the girl.

"Let's get potato chips."

"Okay. A hot dog and a bag of potato chips, please."

"What do you want on the hot dog?"

The man and the boy both looked at the girl. She wrinkled her nose so that her glasses would slide back up.

"Nothing."

"Nothing? You mean raw?" asked the boy.

She looked at him indignantly. "It's not raw. It's just plain."

"Not even catsup or something?"

The man threw down the dish towel he had been wiping the counter with and walked away.

"Hey," said the boy, but the man ignored him. He

walked around a tall rack of open shelves that extended from the floor to the ceiling. It was partially filled with wire baskets of people's clothes.

There was another counter in the wall of the concession stand facing the back row of the changing cubicles. An old man and a woman were standing there in their bathing suits. The man threw the wire baskets with their clothes on the rack of shelves. He gave them each a safety pin with a little brass tag on it. The boy and girl watched silently until the man came back.

"A plain hot dog and a bag of potato chips," said the boy.

They carried the food to the row of railroad ties by the parking lot. They didn't want to sit by the people on the beach. They took bites from the hot dog, each biting from an opposite end. It didn't taste very good.

"There's one bite left," said the girl. "You can have it."

He didn't say anything. He was watching a boy and a girl at the back of the concession stand waiting for someone to take their clothes. They were both very tan and had long blond hair. They didn't mind waiting. The girl leaned on the counter, and her boyfriend let his hand slide down over the seat of her swimsuit. She slapped his hand away and then leaned over again.

"Do you want to get some clothes? I mean, some real clothes? If we're going to walk back to camp we need some shoes."

"How do we do that?" she asked, putting down the bit of hot dog carefully on the railroad tie so that it wouldn't roll. She tore the corner off the potato-chip bag with her teeth.

"There's only that one guy at the hot-dog stand. He has to sell stuff and take people's clothes by himself. If you kept him busy I could grab a couple of baskets."

She thought of them running across the lawn carrying the baskets, the fat pink man screaming at them.

"That's crazy."

"No, it isn't. I could do it."

The girl saw that he was still watching the couple waiting to check their clothes. They looked like an advertisement for shampoo or sugarless gum.

"All right," she said, her eyes going narrow. "What'll I do?"

"How much money have we got?"

She counted their change. "Sixteen cents."

"Is that all? I thought we'd have enough for you to buy something else."

"There was the tax."

"Well, couldn't you pretend to buy something?"

"I don't know. Wait a sec." She picked up a bit of cinder and the last bite of hot dog. She rubbed the cinder into the pink meat. "Okay," she said. "Where shall we meet afterward?" She was holding the bit of hot dog in the flat palm of her hand, as if it were not quite clean, and frowning at him seriously.

"Behind the changing places."

"Okay."

He watched her get up and start toward the concession stand. She was almost marching. He thought he should have picked somewhere else to meet in case they had to run, but it was too late now. He stood up and wiped his hands on his pants. They were wet and sticky.

There was a little boy ahead of her buying a popsicle, so she had to wait. The man frowned over the little boy's head. He looked first at her and then at the piece of hot dog in her hand.

She couldn't see what was going on at the other counter because the man was in the way, and she was afraid to try and look around him. She realized suddenly that she should have waited until the man had taken the wire baskets from the blond couple. The boy wouldn't be able to grab anything if they were standing there. It was too late. The little boy in front of her moved away, pulling the sticky wrapper from his popsicle. The man didn't ask what the girl wanted. He just looked at her.

"There was a rock in my hot dog," she said. Her voice came out tight and squeaky.

"Sure. Beat it." The man picked up a dirty wet cloth and started wiping the counter.

"There was."

"Sure there was. And you want your money back."

"No."

The man looked up, faintly surprised.

"I want another hot dog. This one wasn't any good."

The blond couple came out from behind the concession stand. The boyfriend was trying to fasten a safety pin with a brass tag to the strap of the girl's swimsuit. She was watching him look into her top and smiling.

"What is it with you guys that the bug is always in the last bite?" said the man, starting to turn away. He was bored. His look suggested that he had heard it all before.

"It was! And it wasn't a bug. It was a rock!" She heard herself shouting, trying to hold his attention. "You give me another hot dog or I'll call the cops."

"Sure. You do that . . ." The man was looking at the blond couple, a puzzled look taking shape on his face. He was going to wonder in one second where they had got their brass tags.

"I want one!" she shouted, slapping the counter with her bare hand as hard as she could. It made a terrific noise, and her arm tingled. She and the man looked at each other, shocked.

"For Pete's sake, give her another hot dog," said someone behind her. It was the man who had been putting up the volleyball net. His kids were swinging on his hands, looking at her.

"That girl has on a funny swimsuit," announced the little girl, who was short enough to see.

The counterman didn't pay any attention. He was leaning past her, talking to the man. "Listen, bud. If you knew the grief these kids give me . . ."

The girl walked stiffly away. She knew she should

stay. She knew she hadn't given him enough time. She knew it.

He was standing hunched over two baskets behind the changing stalls.

"What took you so long?" he asked, shoving a basket with a pink sweater on top into her hands.

"How did you get them? Weren't those people there?"

"Yeah. I just went behind the counter and gave them some tags. They must have thought I worked there. That's her stuff." He pointed at the basket. "Hurry up and get changed." He scuttled away, darting into an empty stall.

He dressed quickly and then waited with his door open a crack until he saw her come out of a stall down the row. She was wearing high tops, baggy designer jeans, and a pink sweater over a T-shirt that said *Milk Bar*. She stood very straight, and when she turned toward him, she smiled nervously.

They walked without speaking across the parking lot. His legs weren't working too well. He wanted to break into a run, a screaming gallop into the trees. It wasn't because he was afraid. He was almost rigid with pent-up excitement. It felt like joy.

She stopped and scooped up the bag of potato chips she had left by the railroad ties, and they walked together down the drive toward the highway, eating the chips one by one.

When they were out of sight of the concession stand, he went through his pockets. He found a quar-

ter and a small brown spiral notebook with the stub
of a pencil stuck in the binding. Inside were some
addresses. He tore these out because they made him
feel uncomfortable, but he put the notebook back in
his pocket.

"Did you find anything?" he asked.

She frowned. "There was her wallet and watch, but
I left them in the basket."

"That's okay," he said quickly. "We don't need
them or anything. We shouldn't take stuff we don't
need."

"Wait a sec," she said, and pulled something from
under her sweater and shoved it into the bushes. It
was the underwear that she had made out of the old
T-shirt at the cottage.

"I didn't want anybody to find them," she
explained.

"Did you put on her underwear?" he asked.

"Sure, didn't you?"

"No." He had shoved the boyfriend's jockey shorts
under the seat in the changing stall. They had been
warm, and he hadn't even wanted to touch them. "I
just didn't want to."

"Hers were clean and everything." She walked
beside him, smiling to herself. She wouldn't look at
him.

"What are you smiling about?" he asked.

She looked around. The road was empty. The sun
was shining through the leaves overhead and lying in
flat puzzle pieces in the dust. She unfastened her

jeans and pushed them down a little. She was wearing tiny bikini panties. They were pink and mostly lace.

"Hey, you dope! Pull your pants up!" he said, flapping his hands.

She didn't mind. She fastened her jeans calmly, still smiling. As they walked, they bumped shoulders. He thought he would like to hold her hand, but he couldn't because she would think he liked her in that way. So he bumped her shoulder again.

"Hey," she said, bumping him back. They began to run down the road, careening off one another through the patches of shadow and sun.

The Bus

"HOW MUCH have we got?"

The girl counted the change again, although they both knew. "Forty-one cents. That must be enough for something."

"I don't know. We can probably buy Life Savers or something."

They both looked across the road at the gas station. It was old, with wooden siding that had settled into wavy lines. Someone had hung a large metal sign over the pumps. It said COLD POP.

Two bright-yellow school buses were parked on the highway shoulder. Kids were lined up at the restrooms stuck out in the pines to one side of the station. A few were dancing around the pumps, the headphones of transistor radios clamped over their ears. Most of the kids were black. A white man in Bermuda shorts with a clipboard was leaning through the open door of one of the buses, talking to someone they couldn't see.

"Shall we wait until they go?"

"No. I don't know why we should. Maybe it's better this way. No one will notice us in the crowd."

The inside of the station was crowded with more kids. Some of them were feeding quarters and dimes into a candy machine. They were watching bags of chips and cookies spiraling out on metal coils behind the glass front. A man in greasy overalls and a cap that said *Corn King* was watching them unhappily.

"You! Cut that out," he said to a tall black teen-ager who was slapping the machine with his hand.

"This mother just ate my quarter."

"I'll give you another. Just don't hit the machine."

The boy tried to work his way through the crowd. People bumped him, not seeing him. He felt invisible. He couldn't find the beginning of the line where he could wait his turn to use the machine. There didn't seem to be one. Someone gave him a nudge, and he was about to nudge back when the girl caught his hand and pulled him toward the door.

"Hey. What's wrong? I didn't get anything yet."

She jerked her head toward the window. Through the dusty glass he could see that a police car had pulled into the station. Behind it was the gray Toyota Land Cruiser that belonged to the camp. As he and the girl watched, Margo Cutter got out of the Toyota and went up to the police car. She leaned over so she could talk to the policeman inside.

"Come on. We have to get out of here," said the boy.

"Where?"

"We'll get into the woods out back. Let's go before everybody leaves."

They slipped through the door, trying to keep the other kids between them and Margo. It wasn't too hard. Most of the kids were bigger than they were. The man with the clipboard blew his whistle, and slowly the crowd began to meander toward the buses.

Margo had turned around and was looking in their direction. She was squinting into the sun, and put her hand up to shade her eyes.

They kept their heads down, hoping they wouldn't be noticed. The boy took the girl's hand and tried to sidle into the shelter of the trees. The man with the clipboard grabbed his shoulder.

"Come on. Get on the bus and quit horsing around."

The boy ducked his head and pushed the girl up the steps into the bus.

"Sit here," he said, pulling her into the seat behind the driver. He wanted to be near the door in case they had to make a break for it.

Margo had left the police car and begun to walk toward the bus. He had a terrible feeling that they were trapped. He craned his head around, but the back of the bus seemed crammed with suitcases and luggage. They weren't supposed to do that. They weren't supposed to block the emergency exit.

"Hey! What you doing in our seats?" A tall, heavy, black girl was frowning down on them. A fringe of blue-and-pink beads woven into her hair hung down over her eyes. She looked fierce and very angry.

Before the boy could answer, the teenager who had lost his quarter in the machine took the black girl's elbow and steered her into the seat behind them. "Sit down, Tiwanda," he said.

"What you doing? That's Tyrone's seat. I want my seat." They sat down, whispering furiously.

The bus seemed full now. A white man with a gray face was moving down the aisle, counting with his hands, not letting anyone catch his eye. Through the windshield the boy could see Margo. She was standing in the middle of the drive talking to the garageman. The policeman had gotten out of his police car and was walking toward them. He was wearing black aviator glasses. As he walked he lifted his gray straw trooper's hat and smoothed back his hair.

"Forty-two," said the bus driver out loud, coming back to the front of the bus. He put his hands on his hips and frowned down the aisle.

The man with the clipboard climbed the steps up into the bus so that he filled the doorway. "What's holding things up, Wayne?"

"Nothing, I guess. I've got two too many."

"Crap. Are any of you supposed to be on the other bus?" the man with the clipboard yelled.

"That's me, man," said someone behind them. "I'm supposed to be on the other bus."

"No, he ain't, Mr. Carlson. That's me. I'm supposed to be on the other bus with Lydia."

"What you talking about Lydia?" someone demanded. The boy could feel the bus shake as people started standing up.

"Everybody sit down!" said the man with the clipboard. "We've got them all, Wayne. Let's get going."

The bus driver waited until the man called Carlson backed down the steps, and then he cranked the door closed and started the bus. As they pulled past the gas station, the boy could see the top of Margo's head. She was shaking it. In anger, frustration; he couldn't tell.

The bus picked up speed. Dark pine forests stretched off invitingly on either side. A few feet from the road they were so dark that he couldn't see into them. The girl picked at his shirt.

"Where are we going?" she mouthed at him silently.

He shrugged and tried to smile at her. She made a face of mock terror and rolled against him.

Someone was pulling at the back of their seat, and he looked up. A thin smiling black face was leaning over them.

"Hey. How's my man?"

"Okay."

The black teenager smiled and nodded as if that were the right answer.

"That your chick?" he asked, tipping his head at the girl.

"Yes," said the boy.

"Nice."

"Hey, Calvin, you leave them alone," the girl named Tiwanda said from behind the seat. Calvin looked startled and disappeared abruptly.

"Hey, man, what you do that for? I was just saying how do you do."

"Leave them alone, you hear?"

The black girl stuck her head over the seat. She had small delicate ears with gold earrings.

"Here," she said, pushing a can of Coke into the girl's hands.

"Thanks," said the girl.

"That's okay. It's warm." Tiwanda waited until the girl had opened the can and taken a sip. Then she sat back, looking satisfied.

The boy and girl took turns drinking out of the can. It was the first time she had ever shared a glass or a can with someone other than her mother, actually putting her mouth on the same place. It meant that she was getting his germs. She was getting his germs; he was getting hers. She didn't mind. If they had the same germs, she reasoned, they would be all right.

It was warm on the bus. The air smelled of hot plastic and the sweet rich smell of the stuff that some of the black kids put on their hair. He felt very tired. He wasn't hungry anymore. Just tired.

The girl was drifting into sleep beside him, leaning against his shoulder. He turned his head carefully and smelled her hair. He could smell the lake and something spicy and private underneath.

"What are you doing?" she said.

"Smelling you."

"Boy, you're gross," she said comfortably, not taking her head away.

When she was asleep he let his head loll back against the seat so that he could look out the side window. The bus flashed over a bridge and he caught a glimpse of a stream rushing down a hillside over dark rocks and black fallen trees. He thought he saw something moving there. A deer, maybe, with heavy branching horns, running in the same direction the bus was going. He would have sat up, but he was tired, and he didn't want to disturb the girl's head on his shoulder. It was too late to see anything, anyway. Perhaps he would see the deer later.

He began to think again of what it would be like for them to live alone somewhere in the woods. Like deer. People didn't see deer very often, unless they came down out of the woods. They would need supplies. Blankets and things. An ax or something to cut wood. He remembered the cottage where he had broken in. There were other cottages. They could probably find in them everything that they needed. They would keep track of what they took, of course.

Perhaps they could even leave a note with their names. People would know they were out there, somewhere in the woods, but they wouldn't be able to find them. They could build a shelter in some hidden place: a cave, a tangle of trees knocked over by storms. Or maybe it would be best to keep moving, building small, smokeless fires at night. He was good at that sort of thing. At Indian lore. It was about the only thing he had liked at camp. It wouldn't be so hard. Not as hard as going back to camp. Winter, of course, would be more difficult. He could see the girl, dressed in clothes the color of fallen leaves, the smile at the corners of her mouth. He drifted into sleep, his imagination absorbed in dreams of them surviving alone.

He woke up when the bus turned off the highway onto a gravel road. The headlights swept over a weedy verge coated with dust and a sign that said Camp something or other. It was gone before he was able to read it. The girl was still asleep, leaning heavily against his shoulder.

They had drawn quite close to the other bus. Its square yellow back and glowing taillights filled the windshield. Some kids were smiling and making gestures out the window in the rear emergency door. He couldn't understand what they were trying to tell him. It couldn't be important, he decided.

The buses followed the road a long way, descending into narrow ravines filled with mist and climbing out again in low gear. They made a number of turnings and occasionally would cross another minor road. At first the boy tried to keep track, but after a while he gave up. It was going to be hard to find their way back to the highway. Perhaps they wouldn't be able to. He wasn't sure that it mattered.

The bus finally stopped in front of a long low building. Over the double screen door was a single light bulb, around which pale, fragile insects were swarming.

The bus driver turned off the engine and began flipping switches. The bus was filled with harsh light. The girl sat up and stretched, and then hunched over, shivering slightly.

"Where are we?" she whispered.

"I don't know. It's a camp of some sort. We'll get off when the other kids do and then just walk away. It's dark. Nobody will notice."

She nodded and leaned forward, trying to see out into the dark through the reflection in the windshield of kids crowding the aisles.

The bus driver had cranked open the door, and the smell of pines welled up the steps.

"Everybody stay in your seats . . . Stay in your seats!" he repeated in a loud voice. "Mr. Carlson will tell you when you can get off. We don't want people wandering around and getting lost."

"Hey, man. How long?" someone asked. "I'm about to piss myself."

The bus driver looked as if he might say something,

but then he got off the bus, fumbling in his jacket for his cigarettes. The boy and girl sat still, listening to the kids talking and laughing behind them.

After a few minutes the man with the clipboard bounded up the steps.

"Okay, ladies and gentlemen, in a minute we're going to get off the bus." The kids whistled and cheered, and he waited until they had quieted down. "Be sure to bring all of your personal belongings. We're going to lock up the buses for the night, and what you don't have you'll do without. Is that clear? Okay, then. This building you see out here is Camp One. That's the dining hall. That's where we'll eat and play games . . ." He paused, turning red and smiling, for another cheer. "Mrs. Higgins is at the south end of the building. That means you turn left when you get off the bus. I'll be at the other. Girls rendezvous with Mrs. Higgins. Boys with me. We'll show you where your cabins are. Cabin assignments are final. No switching around. Okay? Everybody knows their left hand from their right? Okay. Don't forget any of your stuff." He nodded and backed his way down the steps.

The boy and girl worked their way into the line getting off the bus. A fat kid with a pink suitcase squeezed between them, and for a moment he was afraid they were going to be separated, but she waited for him just outside the door.

"Where do we go?" she whispered.

Kids from the bus jostled by them, claiming friends, making plans. He stood still, momentarily confused by the dark.

A tall black girl whirled against them, her eyes shining with excitement. She gathered them both under her thin, elegant arms as if she must hold on to something or fall down.

"Oh, man, did you ever see anything like that?"

She was smiling and looking up at the sky. The Milky Way was spilling coolly through the clean air. "Did you know there were so many stars? I never saw them before. Did you know there were so many?

"I don't believe it. I just don't believe it!" The black girl held up her hands, as if to let the glittering lights run through her fingers. She didn't notice as the boy caught the girl's hand and slipped away from the crowd around the bus.

They walked together straight toward the dark woods. It wasn't far. Just beyond a small shed smelling of toilets and disinfectant, he could see the net of shadows beneath the first trees. If they could get that far, they would be safe. He could already feel the cool breath of the night woods against his face. He no longer heard the campers milling behind them. It was a shock when strong hands caught his arms from behind.

"Hey, man," someone hissed in his ear. "What you doing? Did you think you could just *walk*?"

. . .

The camp parking lot was empty. Maddy stopped her car beneath a sign that said FOR OUR VISITORS and turned off the engine. As it cooled it made irregular clicking noises.

Above her, on a hill covered with dark trees, she could see the roofs of the camp buildings. It would be dark soon. Laura must be there by now, waiting.

Maddy wondered if she should have come. In her first panic upon hearing that Laura was missing, it had seemed the obvious thing to do. Now she wasn't so sure. What if Laura should greet her with that dull puzzled look that came down over her face like a mask, making her fears into something pointless, even ridiculous? Maddy didn't think she could stand that.

Wells had suggested that it might be better to wait. That the long drive might be for nothing. He hadn't been so smooth and bland before he had understood that Maddy had spoken to Laura. He had been a frightened man then, almost incoherent, mumbling about the possibility of a swimming accident, trying to reassure her before she had even understood what he was talking about.

There had been a moment, no more than a few seconds really, when Maddy had thought that Laura had drowned. For those few seconds Maddy felt as if a razor had sliced deeply into her flesh, and she had stared numbly into the wound.

The misunderstanding had been cleared up quickly. The wound had closed even before she had felt the pain. What would it have been like if Wells had called first? She hadn't the courage to imagine.

Maddy sighed and, getting out of the car, climbed the long path toward the administration building. There seemed to be no one around. A pair of campers in white shirts that seemed to glow in the fading light eyed her suspiciously from a distance, and then glided off among the trees. There was no one else.

Inside the administration building was a long counter of yellow wood. From behind the counter a middle-aged woman looked up at Maddy inquiringly. She was deeply tanned, and her thin hair was pulled back from her forehead by the weight of a silver-and-turquoise clasp. Her small mouth was wreathed with sharp little lines.

"I'm Mrs. Golden. Laura's mother. I want to see Mr. Wells?"

"Oh yes. Mr. Bob was waiting for you, but he just stepped out." The woman didn't know what to do with the papers in her hands. She considered putting them on the counter, but then changed her mind and put them on the desk behind her. "I think he's gone to the dining hall. I'll just fetch him." She seemed afraid of being left alone in the office with Maddy.

"Wait a minute. Can you tell me if Laura's come back?"

The woman stopped abruptly. "Oh, I don't think so. Mr. Bob would know about that." She smiled. A small, tight, give-nothing-away smile. She looked at

Maddy as if waiting for permission to go. "I'll just fetch him. All right?"

Maddy waited. There was nowhere to sit down. On the wall behind the counter was an elaborate trophy made of lacrosse sticks and canoe paddles. It was covered with dust and varnish.

A fat man came up the steps into the office wiping his mouth. "Just grabbing a quick bite," he said. He was wearing a Hawaiian shirt, and half-frame reading glasses dangled from a chain on his chest. "Mrs. Golden? I'm Bob Wells." They shook hands. "And this is Miss Haskell." He waved at the woman who had bustled back into the office behind him, nodding and smiling as if it was to see her that Maddy had driven up from the city.

"She's camp secretary. Some of the campers seem to think she's their mother." Mr. Wells and the woman beamed at one another.

"Well! Come into my office, and we'll see if we can get this business straightened out." He led the way behind the counter and through a doorway into a small room decorated with more trophies. It seemed important to the secretary that she go in front of Maddy.

"Miss . . . Haskell, is it? She said she didn't think Laura was back," Maddy called after Mr. Wells as she picked through an obstacle course of furniture. She had an irrational idea that he might escape from her. Disappear through some hidden door.

Mr. Wells didn't answer at once.

"Sit down, please, make yourself comfortable." He himself sat down behind a desk and put on his glasses. He laid his hands palms down on a clean, fresh blotter.

"No. She's not back yet." He looked at Maddy reproachfully over his glasses.

"But I don't understand," said Maddy, beginning to feel frightened. "It's hours since I spoke to her. Where can she be? I mean, what can have happened?"

"Now, now, now," said Mr. Wells sharply. "I don't think we should be too worried yet. We know they were safe when you talked to her. That's the important thing. We don't know where she was calling from, or even where they came ashore. It might take them some time to get back to camp. I really expect them any time now, Mrs. Golden."

"But she's only thirteen. Isn't anyone looking for her? Something terrible . . ."

"Mrs. Golden, I notified the sheriff and the ranger just as soon as we knew they were missing this morning. Some of our senior counselors are out searching for them right now." He managed to look understanding and affronted at the same time.

"But why haven't they found her? I really don't understand this."

Mr. Wells looked vaguely surprised, as if she had disappointed him in some way.

"Well," he said patiently, "we have to consider the

possibility that they might not mind making us worry a bit." He exchanged a fruity, knowing smile with Miss Haskell.

Maddy began to feel annoyed. "Listen. Laura isn't like that. When she says she'll be back at a certain time, she is. I left her in your care. I want my daughter back. I want her now."

"Mrs. Golden, no one is more aware of their responsibilities than I am. We are doing all that can be done to find them. I assure you that I am as concerned for their welfare as you are. Now"—he leaned forward, hunching his shoulders to show that he was getting down to business—"did Laura actually tell you that she was coming directly back to camp?"

"No, not in so many words . . ."

"I think you told her that you would meet her on Saturday at the Parents' Weekend."

Maddy looked at Miss Haskell. The woman nodded slightly, as if to encourage a dull student.

Maddy looked back at Wells. "Are you suggesting that she might not come back until Saturday? That's simply ludicrous."

"Mrs. Golden, I think I can say that I know these kids pretty well. They don't always understand how their behavior can upset others. Particularly their parents. Now, I'm sure that Laura is as good a girl as you think she is. Believe me, Mrs. Golden, it isn't yet time to be deeply worried."

"Laura is . . ." Maddy began, and then stopped. She didn't know what she had been going to say. In some way the man had put her on the defensive. As if it were Laura's behavior which had to be justified. She took a deep breath and began again. "What exactly happened, Mr. Wells? I think you owe me some kind of explanation."

For the first time the fat man looked uncomfortable. "Not something that any of us approve of, Mrs. Golden. It was, frankly, a practical joke that didn't work out the way it should have. Completely unsanctioned by the camp and its staff."

"Joke? I know, you said that on the telephone. But what was the joke?"

"Well, it's an old tradition at the camp. It started a long time back. Back when, well, frankly, there wasn't the same attention to camper supervision that we find advisable now." He looked at Maddy to make sure that she understood that this was an important point.

She waited. The man stirred uncomfortably. Miss Haskell cleared her throat, and Wells darted the woman a glance of such ill-concealed irritation that Maddy was taken aback. She knew very little, she realized, about these people with whom she had left Laura.

"You must know, Mrs. Golden," he began again, "that at a large camp like this, with children from all sorts of homes, broken homes . . . all kinds. I'm sure you know that there are always a few campers who don't fit in right away. That doesn't mean that they're unpopular. Far from it." he said hastily, misinterpreting Maddy's stricken look. "These are often children who are deeply admired. The other children want to make friends with them. Make them a part of the community."

"What did they do to her?"

"Sometimes," Wells continued as if he hadn't heard the pain in her voice, "sometimes there are boys and girls who are a bit, well, judgmental about their fellows. And some of the other campers might decide, mistakenly, that things could be improved if a boy and girl were put in a situation where they might realize that we are all just people. That there's nothing wrong, for example, in a healthy interest in members of the opposite sex." Mr. Wells smirked slightly.

"Mr. Wells, I don't understand what you're talking about. What did they do to Laura?"

The man surrendered reluctantly. "Well, they marooned Laura and this boy, Howie Mitchell, out on this little island together. It was to be just for the night. Not very clever, I agree." He raised his hand before Maddy could speak. "I don't think any real harm was meant. It's happened before, back in the bad old days, and I don't think any offense was taken, usually. I think most kids teased in this way would come back, well, a little proud of themselves, actually. There's an old tent platform there. It's perfectly safe. It's just the other campers' way of saying, 'Hey, kids, come on! Get with it!' "

Maddy felt her heart constrict into a small, painful lump. "That," she said, "is the most beastly thing I have ever heard of."

Mr. Wells looked at her, full of compassion. "Mrs. Golden, I fully understand how this must seem to you. And I admit that for more sensitive children it might not be a good idea. And of course there's always the possibility of an accident. Swimming accident, or something like that. That's why I put a stop to this business as soon as I became director. We haven't had an incident like this in years, believe me. But traditions die hard. Some of the campers here are third generation, if you'd believe it."

"I was a goat," announced Miss Haskell.

"What?" said Maddy. She thought the woman had said she was a goat.

"A goat. We call the island Goat Island." She blushed. Maddy understood.

"I'm going to sue you," she said levelly. "I'm going to sue you and this camp right into the ground."

Mr. Wells turned bright red, and his sympathetic expression hardened by a minute degree into something made of wood. "I don't think that attitude is going to help us, Mrs. Golden. The important thing right now is that we get Laura and Howie back, safe and sound."

Maddy looked at him silently over his desk. It seemed strange to her that she had not realized at once that this man was her enemy.

"Now, about the boy." Wells began to fuss with some papers on his desk, as if the boy were some last, minor detail. "I don't think you have anything to worry about from that direction. He's a nice boy. Quiet, wouldn't you say, Miss Haskell?"

Miss Haskell agreed. Howie was very quiet.

"No, you don't have to worry about that, Mrs. Golden. Howie wouldn't harm your daughter." He smiled as if it were, really, only a joke. "He's about two inches shorter than she is, for one thing. You know girls at that age mature more quickly."

Maddy hadn't worried about the boy hurting Laura. She had never even thought of such a thing. In all her imaginings of what might happen, this had eluded her. She looked alertly from the man to the woman, wondering what other horrors might be concealed.

She heard Wells explain that they were trying to notify the boy's parents. She understood that there was some difficulty about getting in touch with them. They were in Turkey. Digging, excavating. She wondered vaguely if they were some kind of engineer.

Wells and Miss Haskell were standing now, so Maddy got up. There was nothing more she could learn there. They would be in touch, of course. Miss Haskell explained about the reservation she had made at a local motel. She was sure that Maddy would be comfortable.

"Perhaps Mrs. Golden would like to eat with us

in the dining hall tonight. What's the menu, Hilda?"

Miss Haskell looked doubtful. "Corned-beef hash, I think."

"Ah! Cat's vomit. That's what the campers call it. Cat's vomit." Mr. Wells smiled at Maddy. She was afraid he might wink at her.

The Dining Hall

IT WAS the teenager named Calvin who held him, squeezing his arms just above the elbow as Bryce had done.

The girl had faded into the shadows, but when she saw that he was caught, she came out and stood beside him.

"Let us go," the boy said. "We're not hurting you."

"Oh, man, where you going to go to? This is the wilds!"

The boy twisted in Calvin's hands. He was surprised when Calvin let go at once, backing off and holding his hands up. "Okay. Be cool."

The girl Tiwanda was standing close by, watching

from under her fringe of beads. She did not look excited or angry. She looked sad.

"Okay now. Why you running from the Man?"

"Who?"

"The Man. The cops. Back at the gas station."

They had been noticed. The boy had felt invisible, but Calvin had seen them and understood what they were doing. It had been a mistake to leave the woods and go into the gas station. People might see you, think about you, even if they didn't seem to.

"We broke into a house and took some stuff."

Tiwanda's face bunched up in distress.

"Oh, man . . ." she said.

"We had to! We're going to pay them back."

"That's okay," said Calvin. "That's okay. I understand. People shouldn't leave their houses lying around, right?"

"Oh, Calvin, I don't know," said Tiwanda. "I think we better tell Mr. Carlson."

"Don't do that," said the girl.

"Yeah, what's the matter with you, Tiwanda? Carlson would just send them back. They're running, can't you see? Ain't nobody ever run from nothing."

"But it's dark out there." Tiwanda looked into the woods with real fear.

"We're not afraid," said the boy.

"Oh, honey, there's wolves and bears and stuff out there. We can't just let you go. She's scared. Don't you see?"

The boy looked at the girl. Her dark hair was coming down over her face, concealing her eyes. She wouldn't look up at him. He wanted to tell her that it was all right, that they would be safe out in the dark, but he didn't know how to begin. The idea seemed so simple to him, and yet so difficult to explain.

"Look," said Calvin. "Why don't we just keep them with us for the night. We can decide what to do in the morning. Nobody would care. They might just have signed up at the center at the last minute. Nobody knows everybody, not even Carlson. Who's in your cabin? Could you make it right?"

"I don't know," said Tiwanda doubtfully. She looked at the girl. "Where are you running to? I mean, have you got somewhere to go, or are you just running?"

"We're going to meet my mom. On Saturday. In Ahlburg."

"Ahlburg? Where's that?"

"It's a town. It's near here."

"Why don't your mom come get you right away?"

"She couldn't. She . . . she wanted to, but she had to work."

Tiwanda tilted her head back and looked at the girl skeptically. "That don't seem right," she said. She reached out and brushed the girl's hair away from her face. "Is that the truth, honey? Or are you just putting me on?"

"No, it's true. It's really true."

Tiwanda wrinkled up her nose and stared out into

the dark. Behind them they could hear doors opening and closing, people talking and laughing.

"Come on, Tiwanda," said Calvin. "What's the big deal?"

"Well. All right," she said. "For tonight, anyway. I'll take her. Susie Burns is in my cabin. She's going to make a fuss."

"That's okay. Just lean on her a bit. What are you guys called, anyway?"

They wouldn't say. They stood waiting to see what Calvin would do next.

"Oh, man, you are sly. Don't trust nobody. That's okay. You think it over. Here," he said to the girl. "You go with Tiwanda. Clyde here and me will meet you at the dining hall for supper."

"We're supposed to stay together," she said.

Calvin laughed. "You're cane sugar, you are." He bent over her so he could see into her face. "You can't stay together tonight, don't you see?" he explained. "Carlson's got us all segregated. Boys and girls. Tiwanda can slip you in with her all right, but I think somebody might notice if Clyde's there, too. You get it?"

As they turned back toward the buses, they saw that a boy was standing in the light coming from the latrine, watching them. He was close enough to have been listening, yet no one had noticed him. He was very pale, with pale hair and eyes. He had long arms and was dangling a white suitcase in front of him.

"Hey, Pardoe," said Calvin. "How's it going, man?"

The pale boy didn't seem to think Calvin's question needed any answer. He lifted his head slightly and pointed with his chin.

"Who are they?" he asked. His voice was soft and dark, like a bruise.

"Hey, Pardoe, you know them."

"No, I don't. I never seen them before."

"What you mean you never seen them? They're hanging round the center all the time. This is Bonnie and her brother, Clyde."

The pale boy looked at them, thinking. It wasn't pleasant to watch him think. His face was very still and gave nothing away.

"Right," he said finally. He turned, pushing his suitcase in front of him with his knees as he walked away alone.

"Come on," said Calvin. "Let's move. Don't worry about Pardoe. He's got to know everything, but he never gave anything away."

"You stay away from him, you hear," Tiwanda whispered to the girl. "He's no good. No good at all."

The girl helped Tiwanda carry her suitcases to one of the cabins. She had a big suitcase and a small one and a square vanity bag. They were all light blue.

As they opened the door they could hear people laughing and talking inside.

"How we supposed to unpack?" someone was saying. "There's no place to put anything. No closets, no nothing. How are we supposed to hang up our stuff and get the wrinkles out?"

It was the pretty girl who loved the stars. She was standing between the bunk beds holding a red silky blouse. When Tiwanda and the girl stepped inside she smiled.

"Hey, Tiwanda, who's your friend?"

"This is Bonnie. She's staying with us tonight."

The girl who loved the stars nodded slightly, her smile turning thoughtful. The other girls stopped what they were doing and looked at the girl. It was very quiet in the room. A miller moth which had followed them inside blundered around the light bulb hanging from the ceiling.

"There aren't enough beds," said a small plump girl with a loud voice. She was sitting cross-legged on one of the top bunks looking down at them. "There're seven people and only six beds."

"She's my guest, Susie. Bonnie, this is Susie Burns. I think maybe I mentioned her to you."

Susie tried not to look at the girl. "Guest? What do you mean, guest? Where's she going to sleep? She's not supposed to be here."

Tiwanda put down her suitcases and walked over to the bunk where Susie was sitting. She laid her big arm alongside the girl's legs.

"She's going to sleep with me. Does that bother you, girl?"

The plump girl flushed. Bright-pink blotches appeared at the corners of her mouth.

"She's not supposed to be here," she repeated. "She'll spoil everything. She'll get us in trouble."

"She won't get you in trouble, Susie, because you don't know anything. Ain't that right?"

The plump girl wouldn't answer.

"It's okay, Susie," said a white girl with black hair and bright-red lipstick and nails.

"Just tonight?"

Tiwanda nodded slowly.

"Oh, all right." Susie flopped over on her side as if she didn't want to see any more.

"Hi," said the girl who loved the stars, coming close. "I'm Lydia."

"Hi."

Lydia looked down and bit her lip, as if she had something embarrassing to say. The girl waited, wondering what had been found wrong with her. Had she already broken some rule or other? Or was Lydia going to tell her in the nicest way that it would be better if she just disappeared?

Lydia took a deep breath. "You want to borrow my comb?" she asked.

The dining hall was one big room filled with picnic tables. To one side the man they called Mr. Carlson was taking white cardboard lunch boxes out of a big aluminum container and passing them out to a line of kids. Behind him was a large institutional stove, where a gray-haired woman was ladling cocoa into white mugs. The room was chilly and smelled of fried chicken and chocolate.

Tiwanda and the girl found the boy sitting with Calvin and some other kids near the door. They were eating chicken and coleslaw out of little plastic containers.

"Sit here, Bonnie," Tiwanda said, "I'll get us some supper."

The girl wondered if there would be only enough of the little white boxes for the people who were supposed to be there, but no one else seemed worried.

She sat down next to the boy, sliding close enough so that their arms touched. He didn't say anything, but he smiled at her so that she knew he was glad she was there again. He didn't want to interrupt Pardoe, who was explaining what a kid should do if he had no money.

"You find some store like K Mart or Woolworth's," he was saying, "then you look around for some wastebaskets outside. Act like you're looking for cans or bottles, but what you really want is a bag from the store with a receipt in it. There are always some around. People buy something they want to use right away, and they throw away the bag, and they forget about the receipt that was stuck inside. They don't want it, anyway."

It was a complicated plan. It involved stealing items

from the store and trying to exchange them for money using the receipt.

"Oh, man, that don't work," someone said. "They've got a code telling what the stuff is, right there on the tape."

"That's right," said Calvin. "And they staple the bag shut, so you have to tear it to get stuff out. You take up a bag that's been tore and they'll bust your ass."

Pardoe smiled, as if nobody could understand. "It doesn't matter," he said in his soft voice. "You just have to look right. Like your mom is going to call up and complain if they don't treat you nice." He turned his flat eyes on the girl. "She could do it."

Everyone looked at her. It made her nervous. She hadn't thought that Pardoe had noticed her. She didn't want him to think about her. When he smiled, the skin at the corners of his mouth folded into dry little wrinkles.

"No, she couldn't," said Tiwanda, who had come back with two boxes of chicken. "She's not going to mess with any of that stuff. You hear, Bonnie?"

"Get off her case, Tiwanda," said Pardoe. "What's she supposed to do? Get a paper route?"

"I mean it. You shut up about that stuff. She's not going to do any of it."

Pardoe looked away, smiling dreamily. He seemed very sure of something. So sure that he wouldn't explain it to people who refused to understand.

When they had finished eating, Mr. Carlson got up

and gave a speech. He welcomed them to the camp, and asked them to take good care of the facilities, because it was state property and that meant it was theirs, too. He apologized for the box lunch; Milo promised hot food tomorrow. Everyone whistled and cheered, and a man in a white paper cap stood up and bowed. Then Mr. Carlson explained the next day's schedule. In the morning they could explore the camp and get acquainted. There were tennis courts and a lake nearby where they could swim. The buddy system would be strictly enforced. He pointed out the buddy list by the door. It didn't matter if your buddy wasn't a friend; he or she was still your buddy.

In the afternoon there would be an excursion to the Corraine Caverns. They should be ready to board the buses at one o'clock sharp. Mrs. Higgins would stay behind to hold the hands of those who didn't make the buses. They should bring sweaters and jackets and wear sturdy shoes. No clogs or heels. It had been a long day, and lights-out was at ten o'clock. Until then they could do what they wanted. Keep it decent. And no, he wasn't going to tell them where the lake was until morning.

When Mr. Carlson had sat down, some of the kids got up and began to collect the empty lunch boxes in big plastic bags. Others began to push the tables back against the walls. Someone turned on a large portable radio, and a boy in a windbreaker and a big felt hat began to sketch a few steps of a private break dance off in a corner.

Lydia came over to their table carrying a cup of cocoa. "What's this Corraine Cavern excursion? I'm not sure I want to mess with that."

"You'd love it, Lydia," said Pardoe. "It's a big black hole in the ground. People are always getting lost down there. They never find most of them."

"Don't give me that. Why would anyone want to go down a hole? Even subways give me the willies."

"It's probably interesting," said Tiwanda. "I was in Mammoth Cave once. Mammoth Cave in Kentucky? They had interesting stuff there. Fish with no eyes and underground lakes and stuff. They had these stalagmites that looked like fried eggs and some like a pipe organ. They played music and had a light show. It was real educational."

"Mammoth Cave is where they found these mummies of people who got lost."

"Shut up, Pardoe. There ain't no mummies in there. That's in the pyramids. In Egypt."

"No, man, it's true. There's something about the air in there. These people dies, but they don't rot. They just sort of dry up."

"I was in a cave once," said the boy suddenly. He was sitting up very straight like a little kid and looking at them. The girl noticed that he hadn't eaten much of his chicken. She couldn't understand that, because she was starved.

"What cave was that?" asked Tiwanda.

"I don't remember the name. It's in Greece. It's really old."

"Was it scary?" asked Lydia. "Because if it's scary, I don't want to hear about it."

"No, it wasn't scary. It was kind of—I don't know—weird." He laughed nervously. "There was this god that used to live there."

"God? In a cave?" Tiwanda was scandalized.

"Not God god. But this special sort of god."

"Like the Romans and stuff?"

"Yes. This was a Greek god. People used to worship him. They built this altar out in front of the cave, and they would sacrifice goats and stuff."

"What do you mean? Kill them?"

"Yes. And then they'd cut up the bodies and burn parts of them. This was all in the olden days," he said to Lydia, who was making faces.

"Why'd you go up there? What were you doing in Greece?" asked Pardoe. He sounded insulted, angry, but the boy didn't seem to notice.

"My dad knew all about this cave, but he had never seen it. So we decided to walk up there one day. It was really hard to find, because we just had this old map from a book, and it wasn't right. We had to walk miles and miles, and it was really hot. I thought we were going to die before we got there."

"What was it like?" Lydia asked. "Did it have blind fish?"

"No, it wasn't anything like that. It was like a mouth. And it got really big inside. Like the inside of an airport terminal. Only it was dark at the back. There weren't any lights."

"Did you see your special god?" asked Pardoe. He twisted his mouth up to show that he thought it was all a joke.

The boy picked up a chicken leg and looked at it. Then he put it down again.

"I don't know. Maybe."

Everyone was quiet for a minute.

"Well, what did you see, man?" asked Calvin.

"I'm not sure. I was feeling pretty weird, you know, with the sun and everything. My dad was trying to read these inscriptions on the wall near the mouth of the cave, and I thought I would walk back and see if I could find the end. I had this flashlight and everything, but it didn't work very well, because it had these lousy Greek batteries. Anyway, I was walking back and back and it was getting darker and darker, and I thought I saw something move." He had been holding his hands up to talk with, and now he held them still, just above his shoulders. He was smiling a little.

"Oh, man!" said Lydia. "I thought you said this wasn't scary!"

"That was kind of scary. I was really scared, actually. I turned around and started running, but I couldn't see the light from the opening of the cave anymore. I didn't even feel like I was in a cave. The darkness just went on and on. All over the world, it felt like."

"Oh, man. What happened then?" asked Calvin.

"Nothing really." The boy frowned and looked in

his lunch box. "My dad grabbed me and carried me out of the cave. I must have been yelling or something. We went back later, but we couldn't find anything, but Stephanos—he's a friend of my dad—he said it might have been the god. That some people thought he was still there, but he didn't come out very often because people didn't give him goats anymore."

"It was probably a rat," said Pardoe. "Caves have rats. It was a rat god."

The boy looked at him, but didn't say anything.

"I don't care if it was Santa Claus," said Lydia. "I'm not going in any cave tomorrow. No way."

People began to fidget, tapping on the table with their hands and looking around. It was as if he had said something that they didn't want to hear. Something that made them nervous.

The girl didn't like that. She leaned against him so that he could feel the warmth of her shoulder through his shirt.

Someone had turned up the radio, and kids were dancing in the center of the room. Mr. Carlson and Mrs. Higgins were sitting with some other adults at a small table, talking and playing cards.

"Come on, Clyde. Let's you and me dance," said Lydia.

"No," he said. "I don't dance very well." He could feel the girl's weight against him. He was very comfortable. But Lydia wouldn't allow it. She caught his hands and pulled him away from the table. He liked Lydia, but he was glad when one of the big kids from the bus started dancing with them, too. The big kid matched his steps exactly to Lydia's, so that they moved together in short slight movements. It was pleasant to watch them. After a few minutes the boy sidled away.

He saw the girl sitting alone with Pardoe at the table. He couldn't see Calvin and Tiwanda. Pardoe was smiling, and the girl was looking at the floor, as if she wanted Pardoe to leave her alone.

"Well, if it ain't Clyde. Hello, Clyde."

The boy nodded once. He didn't know what Pardoe might do, and he understood that he must be careful.

"I was just telling your sister here that it isn't smart to go running around in the woods. People see you. They wonder what you're doing. They might call the cops if they wonder enough. It's better in the city. Nobody cares."

"We're going to meet her mom on Saturday."

"Oh yeah. You're going to meet her mom on Saturday." Pardoe repeated his words as if they were a lesson he had difficulty remembering. He was smiling at the boy, and then his eyes changed so that he was looking through him at the other side of the room.

He turned back to the girl suddenly. "Hey, Bonnie. Look at this." He fished a brass key on a string out of his shirt. It was moist and shiny from rubbing against his skin.

"It's a key. So?" said the boy.

"That's right, Bonnie. It's a key. But do you know whose key? Ever hear of Art Mobling?"

"Yes. He's on TV," said the boy. It was strange talking to Pardoe this way, because Pardoe was pretending he wasn't there and that it was the girl who was asking the questions. It made him feel big and in the way, and at the same time transparent.

"This is the key to his place. Wow. You should see it. I bet you never saw anything like it. It's way up in one of those buildings by the lake. It's got windows all over the place, and all the rugs and stuff are white."

"I don't get it," said the boy, unable to leave it alone. "Why would he give you his key?"

Pardoe turned red, but smiled at the girl as if she had asked the question he had hoped she would.

"He's a friend of mine. A real good friend. He likes to help kids, and I help him out, too. He gave me this shirt. You like this shirt?" He held up his arm in front of the girl's face, but she turned away.

"He'd help you out, Bonnie. Really. You go to him, tell him you're a friend of mine. I'll let you have the key so he'll know you're okay. He'd take care of you. Real well. You wouldn't have to go slumming around in the woods anymore. No strings really. You be nice to him. He's nice to you. That's what friends are for."

Pardoe waited for her to say something, but she simply stared at the floor. She didn't seem able to move. The boy felt as if they were stuck to Pardoe. As if he had been talking to them for hours.

"You like pizza?" Pardoe said brightly. "God, Art and I had this great pizza the last time I was there. Everything on it. Anchovies. You like anchovies?"

"I told you that we were going to meet her mom."

Pardoe turned slowly to look at him. He was still smiling. "You know something, Clyde? You keep flapping that big lip of yours, and I'm not even talking to you. I'm going to get annoyed in a minute. I might have to slap you around a little. Okay?"

The boy felt himself start to tremble. He might even cry. When people said things like that to him, something inside that held his arms and legs together went slack. Pardoe saw it happening, because he was watching.

"Creep," he said. "Come on, Bonnie. Let's go somewhere where we can be alone."

He stood up and tried to pull the girl up, too. He wasn't looking at the boy, because he had decided he didn't matter anymore.

The boy kicked him hard in the side of the knee.

Pardoe made a loud ugly sound and fell down on the floor.

The boy stared at him. He was astounded. He hadn't thought he could hurt Pardoe. He hadn't even expected him to fall down. He thought now Pardoe would jump up like a hero on television and start punching him.

Pardoe stayed on the floor. He was lying on his side and feeling for his knee with one hand. He suddenly looked small and fragile. His face crinkled up like tissue paper, squeezing thick tears out of his eyes.

People were getting in the way, so that it was hard for the boy to see. They kept shoving him behind them, away from Pardoe. He tried to push his way to the front, but someone was holding him back.

"Okay! Okay! Break it up. What's going on?" Mr. Carlson pushed his way through the crowd, using both hands. He wasn't like Mr. Wells. He wasn't afraid to touch people. He grabbed them and threw them aside when they wouldn't move.

"Pardoe fell down," someone said.

"Don't give me that. What happened, Pardoe? Who started this?"

Through a screen of arms and legs the boy could see that Pardoe was trying to sit up. He was no longer crying, but his tears had made red acid marks on his face.

"I fell down," he said. "I've got a trick knee."

Mr. Carlson looked around at Calvin, Tiwanda, and the others. He didn't find anything in their silent faces. They were careful not to look at the boy.

"Okay," said Mr. Carlson in a tired voice. "Party's over. Lights-out in fifteen minutes."

The Cabins

THE BOY let Calvin and his friends hustle him away. He wanted to find the girl and simply leave, running somewhere. But she was gone when he looked for her, and he wasn't able to resist Calvin, who pulled him through the door and out into the night.

He wondered what they were going to do to him. He thought they would probably beat him up because he had kicked Pardoe when he wasn't looking. That was a cowardly thing to do, he knew. That's one of the reasons he was a goat, because he did things like that. Calvin and the others hadn't known he was a goat, but now they would.

He felt bad about hurting Pardoe, too. When Pardoe had been lying on the floor and crying, he hadn't

looked tough anymore. He had looked like a little kid.
That had been such a surprise. The boy could hardly
believe it.

In the cabin Calvin threw himself on one of the
bunks. He was holding his stomach and laughing.

"Oh, man," he said. "We've got a kung fu expert
here. Did you see Pardoe go down? Bang!"

"What's so funny? That ain't funny." It was a
stocky kid named Mason. He slouched over to the
door so the boy couldn't make a break for it.

"What's the matter with you, Mason?" Calvin asked.

"The little creep. He popped Pardoe from behind.
When he wasn't looking."

Calvin hadn't seen that, thought the boy. Now he
wouldn't laugh anymore.

But Calvin was still smiling. "So who says Pardoe
has to be looking?"

Mason licked his lips and looked at the others. "It
ain't fair," he said stubbornly.

"Oh, man, don't give me that knights-and-armor
stuff. You been watching too much TV. Pardoe starts
messing with a bandit, he might get hurt. He ought
to know better."

"What do you mean, a bandit?"

"A bandit, man! They got their own rules!"

The boy didn't understand. Neither did Mason.

"What rules? What are you talking about?" he asked.

Calvin sat up and motioned everyone to come close.
"Listen, children, I'm going to tell you the first bandit

rule." He held up a long, straight finger. "If you see you're going to get popped in a fair fight, don't fight fair." He lay back on the bunk, his arms behind his head. "It's like society, don't you see? They got all these rules that everybody's supposed to play by. But sometimes you see that those rules are going to cut you up. That makes you a bandit. You're a smart bandit when you know you don't have to play that game no more."

The boy still didn't understand very clearly what Calvin was talking about. He didn't think he was really a bandit. But then maybe he wasn't a goat either.

Lydia held her pretty arms up to the cabin ceiling so that her golden bracelets slid down over her elbows.

"Oh, man, that Clyde is so bad! Did you see those eyes? Those are bedroom eyes." She did a little shimmy.

"Shut your mouth, Lydia," said Tiwanda. "He's Bonnie's. You mess with him, she'll mess with you. Isn't that right, Bonnie?"

"Yes," said the girl. "Yes, I will." She was angry and excited. She wanted to hurt someone.

Lydia laughed. "Okay, man. Back off. But if you ever tell him to walk, point him in my direction."

"You be quiet, Lydia," said Susie Burns. "He's too little for you."

"Oh no, he's not. I'll be his sister and his momma.

I'll teach him everything I know. That story about the cave? Did he really go there, Bonnie? Did he really see that special god?"

"I don't know. Yes. I think so." She couldn't listen. She didn't want to think about that now. Pardoe had frightened her. She hadn't understood clearly what he had wanted, but she had been sickened, as if something sweet and unclean had been forced into her mouth.

She watched Tiwanda take off her dress and put it on a hanger. The black girl hung it up on a nail by the door and then put on a white bathrobe. She looked big and safe.

"Tiwanda," the girl asked, "what's wrong with Pardoe?"

Tiwanda sighed. "He's got a bad family history. Don't worry about him. He won't mess with you no more."

"I will kill him."

Tiwanda looked at the girl. She was sitting stiffly on a bunk, her hands crossed between her knees. Her eyes were very big, and she was staring straight ahead.

"I will kill him," she said again.

Tiwanda sat down on the bunk and put her arm around the girl, whose thin shoulders were shaking.

"Someday, honey, somebody's going to. Pardoe's been hurt bad. I don't mean when your boy kicked him. I mean before. He's been hurt bad deep down inside. It makes him all queer. That's why Mr. Carlson lets him come camping with us. He thinks he can fix the hurt.

"Mr. Carlson, he's a good man, and he won't see how bad Pardoe is. But someday somebody's going to see. They're going to say, 'Oh, man, we hurt this thing so bad, we can't let it live. We got to kill it.' But that don't have to be you, honey. That don't have to be you."

"Hey. Come off it, Tiwanda. Ain't nobody going to kill that little son," said Lydia. "Hey, Bonnie, I bet you haven't even got a toothbrush, have you?"

The girl shook her head. She couldn't remember when she had last brushed her teeth. Back at camp, she supposed. That seemed a long time ago.

Lydia was holding out a toothbrush to her. It was new, still in its plastic tube from the store.

"Thank you," she said automatically. She wondered if Pardoe ever brushed his teeth. They had been a thin gray color, she remembered.

"But what will you use? I mean, I can't take your toothbrush."

"That's okay. I've got another. See?"

"Why do you have two toothbrushes?" asked Susie, who was listening carefully to everything anyone said.

"Because you're supposed to. You're supposed to use one and let the other dry out. That way it doesn't collect germs."

"Oh," said Susie. "Yeah. I forgot that for a minute."

There was a small room built onto the back of the cabin, with washbasins and toilet stalls. It was a better camp than the one her mother was spending a fortune to send her to. The girl washed her face and brushed her teeth and then sat down on Tiwanda's bunk and watched the others get ready for bed.

They had nice things, new bathrobes and slippers. They put cream on their faces, and the black girls with cornrows in their hair put on plastic shower caps. They didn't seem to care that you were supposed to rough it when you were camping, so they weren't nearly as grubby as the kids at her camp. It surprised her a little, because she was sure they didn't have as much money. They had enough, she supposed, so that they didn't have to be grubby. They liked things nice.

She began to worry about how she was going to sleep with Tiwanda. The black girl was so big, and she'd never touched a black person's skin. She'd never even slept with anyone since she was little, except the boy, and that was different. She was afraid that there might be some etiquette involved that she wouldn't understand.

She decided finally that she'd take off her shoes and socks and jeans and sleep in her underwear and T-shirt. She thought that would be all right.

When she pushed down her jeans Tiwanda said, "Hey! Where'd you get underpants like that?" She looked very angry.

The girl froze, bent over with her jeans around her knees. She couldn't understand why Tiwanda was so angry. She was afraid they were going to be mean to her.

"I found them," she said finally, faintly.

"Yeah, I bet."

"Come off it, Tiwanda," said the white girl with the bright lipstick. "I think she looks cute."

"Yeah, you would." Tiwanda turned back to the girl. "That's prostitute's underwear. Your mom is going to break a broom on your butt when she sees that. Here." She rummaged in her suitcase until she found a voluminous pair of white cotton underpants. "You put these on. These too," she added, pulling out a pair of pajamas. "I'm not sleeping next to you in your skin."

"I like the underwear," said Lydia. "That's private. You wear what you want there. But, honey, that T-shirt has got to go. *Milk Bar?* You don't want to advertise. Especially what you ain't got."

"She's going to cry," said Susie. She sounded satisfied, as if this was what she had wanted all along.

"Yeah? Well, maybe she's got a few things to cry about. She don't need any help from you."

The girl didn't know why she felt like crying. She didn't feel nervous and scared anymore. Maybe it was because they were nice to her. Nice to a goat. She'd almost forgotten that she was supposed to be a goat. No, not forgotten. She wouldn't forget, and she wouldn't forgive, either. But it didn't seem important in the same way. It was as if it had all happened to some other, littler kid. She was crying a bit for that kid, too. It wasn't the same as feeling sorry for herself, because she wasn't quite the same person. But she still felt bad about what had happened to that little kid.

They turned off the light and got into bed. After a few minutes the gray-haired woman put her head in the door.

"Everything all right in here?"

"Yes, Mrs. Higgins. Good night, Mrs. Higgins."

"Good night."

"Good night. God bless."

The girl was squeezed up against the wall. She could feel Tiwanda's shoulder against her own. It was soft and warm. She felt shy, uncomfortable, and safe.

Tiwanda caught her hand and held it. "What's your real name, girl?"

The girl had to think a minute. "Laura. Laura Golden."

"Laura. That's a pretty name. Your mom pick that out for you?"

"Yes."

"Laura, I want you to promise me something. Just as soon as you get to town tomorrow, you call your mom. You call her and tell her that she's got to come get you right away. I don't care what you say. Anything that will make her come. You promise me that?"

"Okay."

"Say, I promise."

"I promise."

"Do you have any money?" Tiwanda asked.

"No. Forty-one cents."

"That's not enough. I'll lend you some. But you pay me back."

"Okay. Thank you."

"You're welcome. Maybe I can sleep now."

But Tiwanda didn't go to sleep right away. The girl could feel her lying awake, her eyes open, thinking.

"What's your boy's name?" she asked.

"I don't know," said the girl. It was a surprise to her, but it was the truth. Back on the island she hadn't wanted to know, and then it hadn't seemed to matter. She would have to ask him, if she could remember to.

Tiwanda grunted as if she wasn't surprised.

"You like him a lot, don't you?"

"Yes."

"He's not going to get you in trouble, is he?"

"No. He takes care of me. We take care of each other. That's why we have to stay together."

Tiwanda sighed and let her hand go. "Don't I know," she said. "Don't I know."

The boy woke up while it was still dark. He lay very still on the pallet of extra blankets that Calvin had fixed for him. He was listening. There was no sound but that of the others breathing in their sleep. So it had been just a dream.

He had been dreaming about the cave. In the dream it had not been dark. There had been a light down below him so bright he had not been able to see into it. He had walked through the light and emerged in a wood. It was not the dark pine forest around the camp. The trees were olive trees. A wind from the sea lifted their leaves, flashing their silver undersides. The sun was bright and warm, and the air smelled of salt, spice, and the faint acrid tang of burning charcoal. Something was moving among the trees. He could see it out of the corner of his eye, but when he turned to look, it slipped away. At first he thought it was the girl, but then he became aware that she was standing next to him, holding his hand.

"Do you see it?" he had asked. "What is it?"

She said something, but he couldn't understand her. There was something wrong with his ears. They were thick with a kind of roaring silence.

Awake, he tried to think what she might have been saying. He couldn't understand. Had she been frightened? He wasn't even sure of that.

When he knew that he wouldn't be able to go back to sleep, he got up. He wrapped himself quietly in one of the blankets and went out of the cabin. The air was cool and fresh outside. He remembered that he hadn't eaten much supper, but he still wasn't hungry. He was proud of that. He thought it meant that he was getting lean and hard, so that they would be able to survive.

He found the cabin where he thought the girl must be staying and sat down on the steps outside. He scratched lightly on the screen, but there was no response. She must have been sleeping. He knew that he couldn't go in and look for her, but that was all right. He was close enough for the moment.

He leaned back against the screen and listened to the dark wood. Somewhere out in the brush something big and heavy was moving around. He could hear twigs and branches crushed and leaves rustling. The sound would stop occasionally, as if the creature itself were listening, and then begin again.

The boy sat very still, but he wasn't afraid. He knew that he wouldn't have to go into the dark alone. She would come if they had to go. It was a relief in a way to know that she was asleep and couldn't hear it. Soon he would be able to go back to the boys' cabin and sleep himself.

When they had been getting ready for bed, the boy had seen that Calvin's arms were marked with small round scars, like bullet holes. They weren't bullet holes. They were burns. Calvin's father had made them with a cigarette when Calvin was little.

The boy couldn't understand how someone's father could do that. Calvin had said that there were some things you didn't want to understand. Anyway, the man was dead.

The boy wondered if Calvin's father was the sliced-up man in the Museum of Science and Industry. He could have been. He probably wasn't, but he could have been.

It would have to be a man and a woman that nobody cared about. They probably hadn't even known each other. If they had known each other and cared, then they might have been able to stop it from happening.

He could still hardly believe that there were people who would cut someone up this way and put them in a glass case, even if the man and woman were dead and no one cared. But he knew now that there were people like that.

He wondered if Pardoe would be sliced up someday. It was possible. He wondered if they would stop when they were, say, halfway through. He pictured Pardoe's body being run through a big machine like a meat slicer. There would be half a body, and then the rest in layered slices.

They might think, This is a terrible thing we are doing, but they wouldn't be able to stop. It would be too late.

She found him the next morning sitting alone and slightly apart at breakfast. He was eating something white and fluffy, covered with syrup. He ate very neatly, like a cat. She felt a sudden raging tenderness toward him. She was so glad he was there. She wanted to roughhouse; to throw her arms around him and wrestle him to the ground. She bet she could do it. She was bigger than he was. She couldn't, of course. He wouldn't mind, but the other kids would think they were crazy. She contented herself with sliding along his bench and bumping his hip with hers as hard as she could. He smiled at her and bumped back.

"Yuck!" she said. "What's that?"

"Grits. It's made out of corn. Did you ever have it before?"

She shook her head.

"Me neither. It's pretty good, though. You just put lots of syrup on it. It's Milo's specialty. You want some?"

"I don't know. Can I try some of yours?"

"Sure. This is my seconds, actually." He gave her his spoon and leaned his head on his fist so he could watch her eat. He couldn't seem to stop smiling.

"That's a pretty shirt," he said. He reached out and touched the silky red collar.

"Yeah. Lydia gave it to me. She said my T-shirt was common. You know, *Milk Bar*." She made a face.

He didn't understand at first. He had to think about it.

"Hey," he said. "Is that really what it means?" He wondered if someone had tricked the blond girl at the concession stand into wearing the shirt. That would have been mean.

"Do you think that girl knew?" he asked.

"Yeah. She had, you know, tits. Can I put on some more syrup? What are you grinning about?" She felt hot and touchy because she had never said that word to a boy before.

"I don't know." He wanted to tell her how important she was, but didn't know how, so he said, "We would have been all right in the woods last night, don't you think?"

"Yeah. I wasn't really afraid. Well, maybe a little.

But we would have been all right. It's better just the two of us sometimes."

"I think so, too. They're nice, though."

"Except Pardoe."

"Yes. I thought they were going to beat me up, but Calvin just laughed."

"Why would they beat you up?"

"Well, I kicked him when he wasn't looking."

The girl shrugged. "He's bigger than you. I should have kicked him, too, but he was so creepy that I was afraid to touch him. Where's Calvin?" The boy scratched his wrist and looked around the dining room. It was nearly full now, but he didn't see the tall black teenager.

"I don't know. He went to find Milo. He thought he could talk him into giving us a ride into town."

"Really? That would be great."

"It's the wrong town, though. It's someplace called Barnesville. I'm not sure how we'll get back from there."

"Listen. It doesn't matter. I promised Tiwanda that I'd call my mother again and make her come and get us. I didn't explain properly before. If I tell her what they did to us, then she's got to come. What's the matter? Don't you think she will?"

"I don't know. What if she doesn't want me to come back with you?"

"Don't worry about it. She'll let you come. If she won't, then I won't go, either. Hey, I ate it all. Shall I go get some more?"

The boy watched her carry the empty plate through the crowd toward the stove. He wished he could feel as sure about her mother as she did. He knew it wouldn't be hard to separate them once they were with her mother. He knew what it might be like: adults holding them by their shoulders, talking over their heads. They might try to stay together, but he didn't think they would be strong enough. They were really strong only when they were alone.

Ahlburg

IN THE morning Maddy visited the sheriff's office. It was in a small addition built onto the front of a house, covered with asbestos siding. It was very clean. The linoleum floor was so shiny that her shoes etched neat, dusty prints.

The sheriff was an old man in a brown knit suit. His manners were dry, precise, and formal.

He didn't think Maddy had much to worry about. Because she had heard from Laura, they were treating it as a case of runaways. Now, he knew that she had heard all these stories on television and milk cartons, but ninety-nine times out of a hundred, runaways showed up safe and sound of their own accord.

The State Police had been notified. They would

check on any hitchhikers Laura's age anyway, as a matter of course. The county juvenile officer had been notified. A Miss Gallagher. There was no point in going to see her, since she didn't know anything.

He expected Laura would turn up tomorrow at the Parents' Weekend, or even at home. That's where runaways from the nearby camps usually went. He hoped she would notify them if that occurred. It was a courtesy they appreciated, and it helped keep their records straight.

There was one thing. A report he thought might be relevant. He began to sort through a pile of pink flimsies on his desk with dry fingers.

"Some personal possessions—clothes—were stolen from baskets at the bathhouse at the municipal beach. The investigating officers were pretty sure that a boy and girl of about the right age were involved . . . Here we are."

He held a sheet of paper at arm's length so that he could read it. "Well. This isn't much help. Green sweat shirt, bathing suit. 'A little fox with glasses.'" The old man smiled at Maddy. "Does that sound like your daughter?"

Maddy stiffened. "My daughter has been badly abused and frightened. I doubt if she has the time to steal things from bathhouses."

"No, of course not," said the sheriff. "These kids were probably pretty experienced. The girl apparently distracted the attendant while the boy did the pilfering. The boy is described as very cool. Not the same class of kids as you have at camp." He tossed the pink slip back onto his desk. As Maddy watched it drift down among the others, she wondered what he could possibly have meant by that.

On the pavement outside the sheriff's office, Maddy stopped and stared up and down the empty street. The day must be got through somehow. She didn't know what to do. A sign over a café next to the motel across the street said EAT. Obediently she crossed the road and went inside.

She sat down near the front window in a booth of quilted red plastic. A waitress in a short skirt brought her a menu. On the menu were large colored photographs of plates crowded with eggs and bacon, enormous sandwiches of three and four layers, and fruit platters incorporating whole melons and pineapples. She felt as if she was being invited to eat herself to death. She ordered cold cereal.

The waitress brought a pitcher of milk and a bowl. In the bowl was a small box of cereal, still sealed. Maddy read the list of contents on the box carefully as she ate. The cereal was largely fiber and of doubtful nourishment. It seemed appropriate somehow.

When the bowl was empty, she remembered that she had not called her office and told them where she was staying. She had left the camp's number, but not the motel's. It was not too important. The camp knew where to reach her in case Laura called, but then she wasn't in her room, and almost at once she became

convinced that Laura had called and because she was
sitting alone in the café she had missed the message.

She paid her bill and hurried back to the motel
with quick, unsteady steps.

There were no messages. The clerk was sure. He
showed her the pad where messages were recorded,
and would have explained further, but she turned
away. She would still call the office. It was something
that she could do.

A young woman in jeans and a patched anorak
caught her arm. "Mrs. Golden? I'm Margo Cutter."

"Is she back?"

"No. We haven't heard anything. Could I talk to
you a minute, Mrs. Golden?"

"I'm sorry, I was just . . ."

"Please, Mrs. Golden. You talked to Laura yesterday, didn't you?"

"Yes. Yes, I did."

"Well, did she say anything about Howie? I mean,
did she actually say he was with her?"

Maddy tried to remember. Laura hadn't mentioned
the boy. She was almost sure of that.

"No," she said. "I didn't know there was a boy involved until I talked to Wells. Is it important?"

"I don't know. Maybe not. The thing is, we don't
even know for sure if they're together. They were . . .
they were taken to the island separately. I know it's a
little island, but they might not have found each other.
I'd just feel better if I knew they were together."

"Why?"

"Does that sound strange? You wouldn't think so if you knew Howie. He's so little and, I don't know, klutzy. I worry more about him than Laura in a way."

Maddy didn't know what to say. This boy, this Howie, didn't seem very real to her.

"I don't mean to scare you, Mrs. Golden, but I don't think people are taking this seriously enough."

Maddy looked at her. What did the woman mean? Did she expect Maddy to be sobbing? Tearing her hair? She felt a sudden surge of irritation.

"I'm sorry, Miss Cutter. I must call . . ." she began, but the woman wasn't listening.

"We just don't know anything! Laura couldn't swim. We don't know how she got off the island. We don't know if they're together. We don't know if someone picked them up, or what. They didn't have anything, Mrs. Golden. They didn't have any clothes or money. I don't understand . . ."

"What did you say?" Maddy's question fell through the young woman's talk into an enormous silence.

Margo looked up at her, her face troubled and frightened. "Didn't Mr. Wells tell you? They . . . they were stripped before they were dumped on the island. They were naked."

Maddy was stunned. How could this have been allowed to happen? She wanted to howl with pain and anger, but instead watched the desk clerk sorting mail with quick, clever fingers.

"The sheriff . . ." She had to clear her throat and begin again. "The sheriff said that a boy and girl stole some clothes at the municipal beach. 'A little fox with glasses,' he said. Does that sound like Laura to you?"

Margo smiled hesitantly. "I don't know. I wouldn't have said . . ."

"I think it must have been. I think it must have been Laura." A little fox with glasses. She had been annoyed with the description when she heard it. Now she found it comforting.

"I was just going to call my office. To see if Laura might have called again. Perhaps you'd like to come up."

Margo stood by the door as Maddy sat on the bed and placed her call.

"Mrs. Pritzer? This is Mrs. Golden. I'm fine, Mrs. Pritzer. Has Laura called?"

There was a pause while Mrs. Pritzer considered the question. "Yes. She did call. Just a short time ago."

"Thank God. What did she say? Where is she?"

"I'm sure I don't know, Mrs. Golden."

"What?"

"It was a person-to-person collect call, Mrs. Golden. I didn't feel that I could accept the charges since you weren't here."

"You didn't . . . But how could you do this? I mean, I don't know where Laura is. Don't you understand?"

"No, I don't, Mrs. Golden. No one has said anything about this to me."

There was nothing Maddy could say. Mrs. Pritzer was right. Maddy had told her nothing. She had explained, of course, why she had to leave work to Mr. Alexander, the head of her department. She had done everything but tell Mrs. Pritzer. She wondered vaguely why she had not. Perhaps it was because she expected the woman to know everything.

She explained that if Laura called again Mrs. Pritzer was to accept the charges. Yes, Mr. Alexander would approve. Mrs. Pritzer hung up promptly, her goodbye a carefully calculated reproof.

As Maddy replaced the receiver she realized that she had forgotten, after all, to give Mrs. Pritzer the number of the motel. Perhaps it didn't matter. If her office should try to reach her they would call the camp. That was where she would spend the day.

"Is there anyone else she might have called?" Margo asked. She had overheard enough to understand.

"What? No. There's no one." No one at all. Of all the people she knew, there was not one that Laura might turn to. Maddy could not understand how she had allowed such a situation to arise.

"I mean, is there anyone at home? In case she calls there?"

"No. An answering machine."

The two women looked at one another, both thinking of that empty apartment in their own way, and then Maddy dialed with trembling fingers.

The machine had recorded several messages. Someone from the office had called with an inquiry concerning certain contracts. There was a reminder about a demonstration for the homeless. In case she had forgotten. She was really needed. Her mind began to go numb as she heard her own mother in San Diego explain in a high, unnatural voice how much she hated to leave recorded messages. Her mother paused, as if wondering why she had called, and then Laura's voice suddenly said, "Mom?"

"Laura?" said Maddy, forgetting. It was only a voice. Laura was not there. Miss Cutter took a step forward, but Maddy motioned her away.

"This is Laura. I'm okay. I didn't tell you before, but I'm not at camp anymore. I'm with this boy. I like him a lot, but it's not what you think. His parents are archaeologists. We can't go back to camp anymore because they did something really despicable to us. What . . .?" Laura's voice changed, no longer speaking into the phone. Faintly, Maddy heard another voice, one she had never heard before. It was soft and urgent. It was coaching Laura. Telling her what to say.

"Mom?" Laura had turned back to the phone. "They said we were the goats, and they took our clothes. I mean everything, even our underwear. They stuck us out on this island, and they were going to sneak up and spy on us, so we left. We really hate them. I mean that. So anyway, we won't be at camp tomorrow when you come up. We'll meet you in the parking lot. He's going to come home with me. His parents are in Turkey and they're not here. So please make it okay with Mr. Wells. This is very important. We've got to stay together. I don't have any more change, so I have to go. I love you, and I'm sorry that I couldn't get adjusted at camp, but they're really despicable."

Margo was watching her. Her eyes were wide and questioning. Her lips moved, shaping a question she was afraid to ask.

Maddy punched in the appropriate code so that the message would be replayed, and gave the receiver to the young woman. When the message was finished, Margo smiled. If she had been able to see that Maddy was reassured, she might have laughed.

"They sound okay. Really okay."

Maddy tried to smile. "Well. At least it's not what we think." She wondered why she didn't feel the relief that brightened Margo's face. Certainly Laura had sounded all right. Her voice had reduced everything to the commonplace. To the manageable. Why was she still so uneasy?

"I just wish we knew where they were. If they had enough to eat."

"I think I know where they are. At least roughly. They've probably broken into one of the empty summer cottages along the lake. There are dozens of them. They could find what they need there."

"Cottages? Can't we go find them?"

"I've already looked. Yesterday."

"But you didn't find anything?"

"Oh yeah. I found eight at least that somebody had broken into. It's the local sport for teenagers around here. I couldn't tell if they had been there. It would depend, I guess, on whether they wanted to be found. Listen, Mrs. Golden, I don't think you have to worry. They seemed to be taking care of themselves pretty well. It might be best just to show up at the parking lot tomorrow."

"Yes. Yes, I know. You're probably right."

She thought of what that horrible man Wells had said—that Laura and the boy might not mind making them worry a bit. She had been so angry that he would suggest such a thing. Now she hoped it was true. It seemed, finally, fair. Lately she had been willing only to let Laura annoy her. There is not much of an investment in annoyance, and no great return. But terror is something else. You find out exactly how much you love someone when you're terrified.

She leaned back against the headboard of the bed. It was covered in quilted satin. When she touched it with her cheek, it felt cool.

"Do you think," she asked, "do you think I should try to take the boy back to the city with us?"

"I don't know about that, Mrs. Golden," said Margo. "I doubt if the camp would be able to surrender custody, just like that."

"No, of course not." Maddy knew that Margo was right. There would be rules and procedures that Laura and the boy couldn't appreciate.

"It would probably be best if they were separated, anyway," Margo continued. "They're feeling very close now, but it's an abnormal situation. They might be developing a dependency which would interfere with their resocialization later."

She sounded like a textbook on child psychology that Maddy had once read. Reasonable, and yet somehow wrong. Maddy's own intuition was that if you found someone you liked and trusted, you held on for dear life.

Margo was adjusting her jacket in the motel mirror, getting ready to leave. The phone call seemed to have restored her confidence.

"And really, Mrs. Golden," she said. "I don't think you'd want responsibility for both of them. You have your job, and well, we don't know what they've been up to. They'll need supervision."

Maddy didn't answer. She was thinking of the boy's voice. It had been attractive, even compelling. Laura had listened. It might not be as easy to pull them apart as Margo imagined.

The Starlight Motel

FROM WHERE they were squatting among the trees
they could see a man loading suitcases into his car.
He kept twitching up the cuffs of his dark-blue suit
to look at his shoes. He was angry because he was
getting mud on them.

"This is really ridiculous, you know," said the boy.
"We're never going to get away with it."

"Shut up. We're not sleeping in the woods unless
we have to. You're sick, anyway."

That was true. It was just a cold, but it was getting
worse. He shouldn't have gone roaming around the
cabins the night before. He wiped his nose on his
sleeve when he thought she wasn't looking. It was
disgusting, but he couldn't go around with snot hang-

ing out of his nose. He wondered if they could use part of the money that Tiwanda had lent them to buy some Kleenex.

When the man had finished loading his car, he went back inside the motel room and turned off the light. He appeared again, leaning against the doorjamb and wiping his shoes off with a towel. He wadded the towel up and threw it back in the room and closed the door. He was dressed very neatly to be doing things like that. He got in his car and drove away.

"There. You see?" said the girl. "He didn't stop at the office. It's one of those places where you pay when you check in. You just leave your key in your room when you leave."

The boy cocked his head thoughtfully. "They always close the door," he said. "They leave the key inside, but they always close the door."

"Yeah. Well. The next one?"

The boy gave a little shiver. "Okay," he said, and started to stand up.

The girl pushed him down again. "You wait here. I'll do it. I look innocent."

He watched her slide off through the trees. Didn't he look innocent anymore? He thought he must look pretty innocent. Still, she was not as grubby. He sighed and settled back on his haunches among the shadowy green leaves. He felt very content. In no hurry. No hurry at all.

A tiny green bird fluttered close to his head. It knew he was there, but it wasn't afraid. It must be because he was sitting so quietly. Or maybe he was losing his human smell. That was an interesting idea. He thought if he sat long enough there among the trees he might just become a part of the woods. He would not mind that. He would like simply to sit and watch for a long time. The bird, the green leaves, even the back of the motel. It was all very absorbing.

Along the balcony which gave access to the second story of the motel a short fat woman appeared, pushing a laundry cart. She was old, with thin, pinkish hair. Her dress was too short, and she was wearing yellow tennis shoes. They must be careful about her, he thought, and promptly forgot.

Another door on the ground floor opened and a woman and a little girl came out. They walked together toward the passage which led to the front of the complex. The little girl was carrying a Cabbage Patch doll, and her mother was smiling at her.

At the entrance to the passage was a Coke machine and an ice dispenser. They stopped in front of the Coke machine, and the mother held the doll while the little girl stood on tiptoe to put some coins in the slot. Her mother dangled the doll by one leg until the little girl looked at her, and then she cradled it in her arms.

A man came out of their motel room carrying a stroller. He unlocked the rear door of a station wagon and put the stroller inside.

The woman and the little girl were walking back to the car now. The little girl was carrying a bright-red can of soda. She held it up for her father to see, and he made a face as if he'd never seen anything so wonderful.

They never looked up toward the woods. They might have seen him if they had looked, but he knew they never would. They didn't care, probably. There might be all kinds of things watching from the woods, but they wouldn't know because they didn't care.

The girl came around the corner of the building. She had put on her pink sweater and was swinging a plastic trash-can liner. He wondered where she had found it and what she was going to do. She walked directly toward the man, who was now putting two suitcases into the car. The boy sniffed, tilted his head back so that his eyes were almost closed, and settled down to watch.

"Mr. Carlson?"

The man closed the tailgate of the station wagon and looked at her blankly.

"Hendricks," he said.

"Oh. Wrong party, I'm afraid. Are you just leaving? I hope you had a pleasant stay." The girl stood in the open doorway of their room, smiling as brightly as she could. She smiled at the man and at the woman, who was strapping the little girl into a safety seat in the rear of the car.

"Oh yeah. Very nice," said the man. "Thanks."

The girl went into the room. It smelled of cigarette

smoke and damp plaster. She became aware that the man had returned and was standing in the doorway behind her. She emptied the wastepaper basket beside the television set into her plastic bag and then looked at him.

"Just checking to see if we forgot anything," he said apologetically.

"Sure. Have a safe trip."

"Yeah. Thanks again."

When he was gone she looked around for the key. She couldn't see it. It was possible, she supposed, that he had left it in the office, but she couldn't think when he might have done that. She went back outside. The man had just started the car. He rolled down the window as she approached. He looked a little annoyed.

"I'm sorry, Mr. Hendricks. Did you forget to leave your key?"

"Clifford!" said the man's wife. She leaned forward so the girl could see her roll her eyes at her husband. The girl tried to smile. She didn't like standing there in the open. She had seen the cleaning lady but didn't know where she was now.

The man was fumbling in his pockets. His seat belt was in the way, and it seemed to take forever. Finally he flushed and passed out through the window a key with a heavy plastic tab.

"Sorry about that," he said, and winked at her. "I bet you came around just to make sure I didn't forget."

"That's right, Mr. Hendricks," said the girl, and winked back. She was proud of doing that. She had never been able to wink before.

"Have a nice day."

From the woods the boy watched her wave to the couple with the little girl and then go into the room. As she closed the door she looked up into the woods where he was hiding. He couldn't tell whether she had seen him. He stayed where he was until the car had driven out of the parking lot. Then he went quietly down from the woods.

She opened the door as soon as he tapped.

"Come in, come in." She grabbed his hand and pulled him into the room. "I'm afraid the cleaning lady will see." Her eyes looked very bright.

"Shall we just grab some blankets and run?" he asked. That had been the original plan. It was what he still wanted to do in a way. He didn't like the motel room. It smelled of other people and felt small and enclosed.

"No. I want to try it. Here." She pushed a plastic DO NOT DISTURB sign into his hands. "Put this on the door. I have to think a minute."

She was studying the telephone when he closed the door again. She was holding the tip of her tongue between her teeth and her stomach was sticking out a little. She looked very serious.

"You don't have to do this, you know. We can just run," he said again.

She grimaced and bounced up and down on her heels.

"Yeah, I know. It probably won't work anyway, but I want to try. Don't look at me. Go stand someplace else."

He turned away. The couple had left the room in a mess. Did everyone do that? Both beds had been torn up, and a wet towel was hanging on one of the chairs.

He went into the bathroom. It was still warm and steamy. He blew his nose with some tissue and dropped the tissue in the toilet.

The mirror over the sink was cloudy with steam, and he wiped it off and looked at himself. His hair was very bushy and curling down around his ears. There was a small sticky green leaf caught in it. That pleased him and he left it where it was. He wished he didn't have to wear glasses. He took them off and smiled at the foggy reflection. Perhaps if he stayed in the woods long enough, his eyes would get better. His ophthalmologist had told him that they would just get worse and worse until he was about twenty, but perhaps he didn't know about the woods.

When he heard the girl pick up the telephone, he leaned his head against the doorjamb and listened.

"This is Mrs. Hendricks in room 47," she said with authority. "We would like to stay on for another night. Is that possible? Yes. Our car broke down. My husband has to leave it at the garage."

The boy felt himself going jittery. She was talking in her regular voice, not trying to make it deep or anything. This is never going to work, he thought. He went over to one of the beds and started freeing one of the blankets from the tangle. They would have to run for it, after all.

"Yes," she was saying. "That would be fine. Goodbye. Thank you very much."

He started to turn around, but she was already on top of him, knocking him over on the bed.

"Hey! What are you doing?"

She grabbed his wrists and tried to pin his arms back.

"Beating you up," she said through her teeth.

He tried to push her off, but she was too strong and heavy. He was surprised at how strong she was.

"Cut it out. You're making me cough. What did they say, anyway?" He could hardly talk, she was squishing him so.

" 'Just stop by the office before you leave.' "

He was so astounded that he stopped struggling. "Really? Is that really what they said?"

"Really. I'm brilliant, don't you think?"

"Yes."

"Say it."

Her face was close to his. He could smell her breath. It didn't smell like flowers or anything familiar. It was a new kind of smell, and it was both pleasant and alarming. He decided he liked it. He was surprised, too, at how warm she was. When you don't touch people very often you forget that they are really warm.

"You're brilliant."

They looked at each other for a moment, and then she rolled off him. "We better get out of here before the cleaning lady shows up," she said.

She was right, but neither of them felt like moving.

"Where did you get the plastic bag?" he asked after a moment, staring at the ceiling.

"Out of a trash can. I thought I would look like a cleaning lady."

He thought of the old woman with pink hair and smiled.

"I wonder if she'll change the sheets," he said. "I mean the real cleaning lady."

He wished he hadn't said that, because the girl sat up abruptly, wrinkling her nose at the bedclothes with distaste.

"Boy, I hope so. Isn't she supposed to? Even if you stay more than one day?"

"I don't know. We could always sleep in the kid's bed. That wouldn't be so bad."

"How would you know? Which one was hers, I mean."

"Smell them, I guess."

"Oh, my God. You are really very very gross. Come on. Let's get out of here. If we don't leave she won't even get a chance to change the sheets."

At the door the boy paused, stuffing the key with its lumpy tag into his pocket and looking around the darkened room.

"Have you got your bag?" he asked.

The girl showed him the paper bag with her underwear and toothbrush. The bag was getting soft and fuzzy from being carried around.

"Let's go," she said. "What's wrong?"

"I don't know. I keep thinking that we're forgetting something."

"How could we forget anything? We don't have anything to forget."

That was true. There was nothing left in the room that might be associated with them. And yet he had a strong sense that something had been overlooked. It must be simply nerves, he decided.

They closed the door behind them and walked boldly together down the row of empty rooms and out through the passage toward the highway.

Barnesville was small and empty, with a main street too wide for the traffic. The sidewalks were cracked and littered with chips of concrete and dust from the road. It didn't look as if anyone ever walked on them. Most of the old brick storefronts were empty. There was a photography studio that someone had opened beneath a granite façade that said FIRST NATIONAL BANK, and they stopped and looked in the windows.

Behind the dusty glass were highly colored photographs of people getting married and high-school students with flat caps on their heads. The girls had round shiny faces, and the boys too much hair. In the center of the display was a large photograph of a young man in a Marine uniform. He had small, sly eyes and was smiling. Underneath was a sign with a black border that said FOR GOD AND COUNTRY. The boy thought it meant he was dead.

At the end of the main street was a new shopping center. Cars and pickups were parked outside a Jewel supermarket and a Firestone tire store.

The girl stepped in front of the boy so abruptly that he almost ran into her.

"You wait here," she said. "I have to buy something."

"What?"

"A comb and some stuff."

He didn't understand what she was talking about.

"But we've only got about four dollars." It was all that was left from the five dollars that Tiwanda had lent them. They had had to break it so that they could leave a message for the girl's mother. "We need it for food."

The girl twisted around impatiently and stared out over the parking lot.

"This is more important," she said.

"I don't get it. What are you talking about?"

"Listen. Give me the money. I don't have to tell you everything." She was frowning and trying to sound angry, but she wasn't succeeding.

"It's for girls," she said, and turned dark red under her tan.

He thought he understood then. Not exactly. It had to do with that business that Miss Crandell had talked about in health class. He hadn't paid much attention. It had all seemed so unlikely and, well, awesome. He hadn't been able to connect it in his head with the girls he knew.

"Oh. Yeah," he said, and gave her the money. While she went inside, he sat down on a mechanical rocking horse by the door. He wondered if Indians had had this problem before there was civilization and everything. They were people, so they must have had to do something. But when they were living in the woods they couldn't just run down to the Jewel. It was an interesting question and he would like to discuss it, but he didn't think she would want to right now.

When she came out she had a package in a brown paper bag, but she didn't offer to show it to him.

"I bought some bananas, too," she said.

"Oh, that's great. I'm getting hungry. Are you?"

She nodded. "Starving. There's a gas station over there. I have to go there now."

This time he didn't ask why.

While the girl was in the ladies' room, he studied a map that someone had pinned up over the cash register. A mechanic who was working underneath a car on a hoist leaned over so that he could watch him through the door, but the boy pretended not to notice.

After a minute the mechanic put down his wrench and came into the office.

"You want something?" he asked.

"I just wanted to see where Ahlburg is," said the boy.

"Here," said the man. He pointed with a blackened finger at a spot on the map. It was hard for the boy to look at it with the man watching him.

"Is that far?"

"About eight miles. Highway 41. That's this road right here. Okay?" The man was waiting for him to go away, so he went outside to stand in the road. He looked down the highway in the direction he thought Ahlburg must be. Eight miles wasn't that far. If they woke up early they could walk it and be in the camp parking lot before noon. This time tomorrow they might be driving in the girl's mother's car back to the city. It seemed so simple that it made him uneasy.

They ate their bananas in a park behind the supermarket. It was small and dusty, with a large cottonwood in the middle and a rickety swing set in one corner. They sat on a picnic table and watched three little boys race around a dusty track on BMX bicycles. Someone had piled up a mound of dirt in the center of the track, and when the boys hit it, they jerked their bicycles high into the air. They seemed to want to fly away, right out of Barnesville.

The bananas were greenish and bitter, but they ate them slowly to make them last. When they had finished, it was still too early to go back to the motel, so the boy got out the small brown notebook that he had found in his pants and they made a list of the things they would have to come back and pay for.

The girl had memorized Tiwanda's address in the city, but the boy wrote it down just to be sure. The five dollars was a loan, and they would have to pay it back. They weren't sure at first what to do about the other stuff the kids at the camp had given them. There was underwear for both of them; Lydia's red shirt, which was probably expensive; and the toothbrush. They decided finally that it would be rude to try to pay them back for these things. Instead they should get them something nice as a present. Maybe even a portable radio to take with them when they went camping again. It would be great if they could do that.

Then they listed the things they had borrowed without asking. It was surprising how much there was. There was first of all the cans of soup and fruit cocktail from the cottage. And the clothes: two T-shirts, a sweat shirt, and a pair of pants. They would also have to pay for the damage to the shutter on the window. They didn't think they should have to pay for the saltines and the ginger ale. Nobody would have eaten them if they hadn't. Still, they decided that they wouldn't act as if it was a big deal if someone asked them to pay.

Thinking about the clothes they had taken from the bathhouse made them both nervous. The blond boy and his girlfriend probably wouldn't want them back now, even if they were washed. It would be embarrassing to have to meet them, anyway. They decided they would just send a money order if they could find out their names. Perhaps the guy at the concession stand would know.

It didn't seem likely that they would ever find the people who owned the pickup with the roll bar, where the girl had taken the change, but they wrote it down anyway because it seemed right. "Pickup: $1.40."

The motel room was going to be expensive. The boy thought it might cost over fifty dollars. The girl looked stunned when he told her.

"Boy," she said. "My mom's going to have kittens."

"That's okay. My dad will pay for it, I think. I mean, when I tell them what happened."

"Really? They won't be mad because we didn't go back to camp?"

The boy thought about it. No, they wouldn't be mad, exactly. His father would be baffled and upset. It would be like when he failed algebra. He could remember his father standing in the kitchen doorway, watching him while he pretended that he knew what he was doing with his homework. His father had looked so upset and, well, helpless. He had felt awful.

It would interfere with his father's work. That was the bad part. Everyone would be miserable, and his mother would sigh and look at her hands in that funny way that meant he had let them down again.

"No," he said. "They'll just feel bad. I always make them feel bad."

The girl was puzzled. She thought of her own mother, who cried a lot and sometimes said things she didn't really mean. She supposed her mother was feeling bad when that happened. But she didn't think that was what he meant.

"Why?" she asked.

"I don't know. They're kind of old. I think it was a shock when I got born. I was an accident, maybe."

He had never told anyone this before, but he believed it. It would explain why he never seemed to fit into his parents' life. They loved him, and they wanted him to be happy, but they didn't know what to do with him. He had to be careful not to get in the way. It had made him watchful.

The girl leaned forward so she could turn and look up at his face.

"Does that make you sad?"

It was an embarrassing thing to be asked. He wanted to giggle and shiver at the same time. He didn't know what to say.

"I don't know. What do you think?"

She folded up her banana peel neatly in her hand.

"Well," she said, "I think it means we have luck. I mean, you might not have been born, but here you are. That's lucky, isn't it?"

He looked at her dark eyes and her wide mouth with the turned-up corners.

"Yes," he said. "That's lucky."

The Restaurant

WHEN THEY got back to the motel, they found the beds had been made up with clean sheets, and fresh white towels had been piled on a chrome rack by the shower. There was even a paper band around the toilet seat that said it had been sanitized for their protection.

The girl decided that they should take showers. He didn't much feel like it, but she insisted. Neither of them had washed their hair or feet since they had left the island.

The boy went first. When he had finished he felt lightheaded, and his nose and throat were parched. He drank two glasses of water and got into one of the beds with his clothes on.

"Hey," said the girl, who was studying the plastic laminated sheet on top of the television. "They have adult movies. Do you want to watch an adult movie?"

"What is it?"

"*Chaste Coed*. That's a joke, I think."

"Gross."

"Yeah. You have to pay extra at the office to have it hooked up," she said after a moment's further study. "So I guess that's out. There's a Benji movie. You want to see that? We don't have to pay."

He nodded and she turned on the television. Then she went in the bathroom to take her shower.

He lay in the bed with his eyes closed and listened to the television. It was funny: before, he had felt hot, and now, under the covers, he felt cold. He thought about the chased coed. He couldn't see what the joke was.

When the girl was finished with her shower, he watched her comb out her hair at the dresser. Her red shirt clung to her pointed shoulder blades as she raised her arms.

The light of the late-afternoon sun shining through the curtains made the room seem like a burrow. A hiding place. She had been right. It was better to stay there than to run around in the woods, he told himself. But the faint uneasiness that he had felt earlier refused to go away. There was something they had overlooked, but his cold made it too hard to think what it was.

When the girl's hair was combed out, she wrapped

it in a towel on top of her head. He had never seen anyone actually do this. It gave him pleasure to watch the casual, deft way in which she did it. He wondered if he would ever learn everything there was to know about her. When she brushed her teeth, she spit out in the toilet and not in the washbowl. That was interesting.

"What's happening?" asked the girl.

"What?"

"On the television."

"I don't know. I was watching you."

"Creep," she said, grinning at him in the mirror.

She walked over to the bed and looked down at him. "Why are you shivering? Are you cold?"

"Yeah. I can't seem to get warm."

"Shall I get in bed with you?"

"Yes, please."

She kicked off her shoes and got under the covers. She piled up the pillows so that she could sit up and hold him against her as they watched the movie. After a while he stopped shivering.

For some reason the movie was difficult to understand. Perhaps it was because they had missed the first few moments or because it had been cut in some way. It all seemed very peculiar. A blond girl and a boy in neat polyester clothes were being chased by a man with slick black hair. Or perhaps they weren't being chased. They never got dirty. They were never out of breath or hungry. They were excited about something, but they didn't seem to be afraid.

Benji was being chased, too, by a large Doberman. Every now and then he did something cute. The movie would stop for a minute so everyone could see what a cute dog he was.

"I don't get it," said the girl after a few minutes. "Do you?"

The boy shook his head. "It's funny, because I think I saw this movie before."

"Yeah, me too. I didn't know it was so boring. Did you know it was so boring?"

"No. I thought it was great, but I was just a little kid, then."

The girl got up and turned off the television. "Tell me some more about Greece," she said, flopping down on the bed again. "Not the cave. Some nice stuff."

"The cave's nice."

"No, it isn't. I mean, it's not bad, but it's so weird. Tell me about some stuff that isn't so weird."

The boy thought for a minute. "Well, once my dad and I walked all the way from Delphi to the sea. I think that was about the best day I ever had."

"Until now," said the girl so quickly they were both surprised. She turned red, but he nodded.

"Until now."

"What was so special about it?" she asked, trying not to sound too interested.

"I don't know. Partly it was doing something with my dad. He was so busy we didn't do much together. Lots of times I would just sit around in hotels and read comics. But we went on this walk for some reason. I forget why.

"We didn't walk on the road. We walked straight down the mountain and through this great grove of olive trees. It was a sacred wood. Back in ancient times. If you killed anything there, that offended the god."

"Was that the god in the cave?"

"I don't know. Maybe. You want to hear something crazy?"

"What?"

"While we were walking in the wood I got this strange idea that he was still there. That's crazy, isn't it?"

"Yeah, sort of. It's weird. Didn't you do anything there that wasn't weird?"

"No, listen. It wasn't weird. I was so happy. Everything was so clear. Do you remember when you first got glasses? When you put them on and you could see?"

"Yeah, I remember that. I read all the street signs when I rode home on the bus from the eye doctor. I read them all out loud. My mom thought I was nuts. I must have thought nobody can read street signs."

"Well, that's what it was like. Only it wasn't just street signs. It was everything. I'd look at a tree, and Oh wow, I'd say. So that's what a tree is. And then I'd look at a leaf . . ."

"And you'd say, Oh wow. That's a leaf."

He was so goofy he made her laugh.

"It's really true," he insisted, but laughing as well. "I could smell everything, too. The sea, the dry grass. Even the sun."

"Come on. What does the sun smell like?"

"It smells like fire. Like a charcoal fire when you can't see the flames anymore."

"No, it doesn't. You know when you've been swimming and you lie down all wet on the float and stick your nose against the wood? That's what the sun smells like."

"Yeah. That, too." He smiled at the ceiling, drowsy and happy. "We followed a river for a while. It was dry. Nothing but white stones. It hurt your eyes to look at it. A river of bones. I wanted to stay there forever."

The girl picked up his hand and studied it, curling up his fingers with hers one at a time.

"Do you think we could go there sometime? I mean together?" she asked. She touched the palm of his hand with the tip of her tongue experimentally.

"Hey. That feels funny."

"Hey, yourself. Do you think we could?" She held up their hands palm to palm. Her fingers were longer than his.

"Of course. We can if we want to. We may have to wait until we're, you know, older."

"Oh yeah, I know that. But we could if we want to. If we don't all get blown up or something."

She suddenly flopped over on her back so that her turban fell off. She didn't seem to notice.

"Do you know something?" she asked.

"What?"

"I should have asked you before, but I didn't."

"What? Tell me."

She took a deep breath and held it for a second. "I don't know your name," she said all at once. She covered her face with her hands and looked at him through her fingers. "That's pretty stupid, isn't it?"

"No, it isn't. It's kind of a stupid name, though. It's Howard. Howie. Your name's Laura, isn't it? I didn't remember at first, but then I did."

"Yeah. Laura Golden. But you want to know something else? That's not my real name. Did you know that?"

"No. What is it?"

"You promise you won't tell?"

"Yes, I promise."

"Then it's Shadow. Isn't that a weird name? It's on my birth certificate and everything."

He laced his fingers over his stomach, considering. "Shadow Golden." He pronounced it very carefully. "I think it's kind of neat."

"Yeah. My mom and dad thought they were going to have a boy, and they were going to call him Sun. You know. S-U-N. It was supposed to be this really subtle joke, but they had me instead.

"They were hippies. My dad still is, but we don't

see him anymore. He took a lot of drugs and did something to his brain.

"You know something else?" She propped herself up on one elbow so that she could look at him. She was getting excited. "I was almost born in a tepee. They were going to have this big party and natural childbirth and everything. But there were complications, so I got born in a hospital. God, my mother would die if she knew I was telling you all this stuff. My mom, the hippie. Can you believe it?"

"Yes. She's probably okay."

"Yeah, she is really. She changed my name when I started school. She was afraid—you know—that I'd have problems."

"It's still your name. Sort of a special name."

She turned toward him suddenly, so that the wet ends of her damp hair swept his cheeks.

"Do you have any secrets?" she asked.

"I don't know. I don't think so." He tried to think. Sometimes he felt as if he was all secrets, but he didn't think there was anything he wouldn't tell her. Well, there was one thing. He hadn't told her about his idea of just the two of them living together in the woods. He wanted to tell her now, but he was afraid to. He wasn't afraid that she would laugh at him anymore. It wasn't that. He was afraid that it would lose some of its magic. That it would just sound queer.

"There is one thing. But I can't tell you yet."

"You can't?" She was disappointed.

"No. It's because it's about you and me. There has to be this special time when I tell you."

"Well. Will you tell me? Sometime?"

"Of course. I promise."

The time would come. Perhaps it would be tomorrow afternoon at her mother's apartment in the city, but that wasn't what he pictured. He saw them walking together up a road into the woods. The sun was shining and birds were singing. It was an old road, overgrown with grass and small trees. Soon it would disappear altogether. It didn't matter. They weren't coming back that way.

When they woke up they were starving to death. The girl got out of bed and peeked out through the heavy curtains.

"Hey," she said. "It's not even dark yet. What are we going to do?"

"I don't know. How much money have we got left?"

She went through her jeans pockets.

"Thirty-eight cents," she said, holding the money in the palm of her hand for him to see.

"We can get a candy bar. I mean, we won't actually starve to death, anyway. It's just until tomorrow."

"I wish I'd saved that banana peel," she said, sitting down on the bed and looking desolate.

"Why? You can't eat banana peels."

"I guess not, but I'm really hungry." She was so

skinny and couldn't get enough to eat. It made him want to do something.

"Come on," he said, getting out of bed and looking for his sneakers. "We'll buy a candy bar and then go look for some change in cars."

"Do you think we should do that stuff anymore?"

"Well, we could write down the license numbers this time. That way we'll know who we have to pay back."

When he had finished tying his shoes, he stood up and looked down at the straight white part in her hair. "You're not sorry we didn't go back to camp?" he asked. The idea made him nervous.

She looked up at him and smiled. "Are you kidding? I'd rather starve."

Before they left she made him comb his hair and gave him a wad of toilet paper to put in his pocket in case he had to blow his nose. She had noticed him wiping his nose on his shirt-sleeve, but she hadn't said anything. What had there been to say?

Outside, it was dusk. There was a smear of gold in the sky where the sun was setting, and the air was turning cold. The boy looked up into the dark wood, but he couldn't see anything. Still, he thought, there might be something there, watching them. It might not mean them any harm, but it might still be watching.

Many of the motel rooms now had cars parked in front of them. As they walked past they could see the shadows of ordinary people moving behind closed curtains. A faint, confident television voice predicted more sunny days.

They didn't notice the old woman with pink hair pushing a broom along the balcony. She leaned over the railing and looked down at them as they passed beneath her.

The streetlights came on as they crossed the dusty parking lot toward the restaurant attached to the motel. They thought they would buy a candy bar there and then walk down the main street again. They were afraid to look for change in the cars parked at the motel.

The restaurant was almost full. As they waited at the cashier's counter for an old woman to pay her bill, the boy watched a man eating a steak. The man had cut the whole thing up into little bits. He was putting them rapidly into his mouth, chewing all the time. The boy looked away.

In Turkey he and his parents would sometimes eat at a café that had set up tables on the sidewalk. A hissing gas lantern had hung over a big charcoal grill. In the white light small boys and girls with dark serious faces walked among the tables offering single roses or squirts of perfume from brightly colored bottles.

He wondered now if they looked so serious because they were hungry.

His father had always waved them away. He had explained that if you bought something from them you were a sucker.

When he and the girl went to Turkey, they would

have money and they would buy. Their hair would be damp with perfume, and they would eat from a table heaped with roses.

The old woman seemed to be taking forever. She had hooked a cane over her thin arm and was fumbling with a black purse rubbed white around the edges.

The girl was watching her closely. At first he thought she was looking at the candy beneath the glass of the counter, but then he realized that she was watching the old creased hands plucking at the purse.

The woman took out a motel key and handed it to the cashier.

The cashier copied the room number from the tag onto a charge slip, and then pointed out where the old woman was to sign.

"Thank you, Mrs. Grogan," said the cashier, snapping the carbons out of the packet of slips. She gave a yellow receipt to the old woman and then looked at the boy. The girl had already drifted away and was studying a rack of postcards.

"Did you want something?"

"No," he said. "No, not yet."

"Did you see that?" whispered the girl when he joined her. She pulled a card from the rack that said Barnesville was the cherry capital of the world and looked at it hard. "She showed them her key and charged it. She put it on her motel bill."

He knew what she was thinking, and shook his head very slightly.

"She's a grownup. An adult."

"So what? We've got a key, haven't we? We could say our dad sent us to have supper and to charge it, if they ask."

"I don't know. They might want to call him or something."

The girl put the card back in the rack, and her eyes swiveled to a baby in a high chair who was pounding a plate of spaghetti into mush with his spoon.

"I'm really hungry," she said.

They sat down at a table near the window. The waitress who brought them their menus was biting her lip to keep from smiling. She had long blond curls hanging down in front of her ears. He couldn't see what was funny, and didn't look up from the menu when she came back with two glasses of ice water.

"What would you folks like?" the waitress asked.

They ordered hamburgers, french fries, and malted milks. They tried not to look at the prices.

"Would you like some pie?" the waitress asked. "The pecan is special tonight." She winked at the boy, and he wanted to say no, but the girl nodded.

"Yes, please," he said.

The paper place mats were printed with puzzles and games, and while they waited they took turns working them with the stub of the pencil from the little brown notebook. The puzzles were really for little kids, but they did them, anyway.

They had a race to finish the hardest puzzle. It was a maze.

"I'm done," said the girl.

The boy looked at her. He was only halfway through. "Hey," he said. "You don't even have a pencil."

"I used my finger." She leaned over so she could look at his place mat. "Yes," she said. "That's the way I went, too."

He couldn't understand what he was grinning about. In a few minutes the cashier would be looking at them and wondering what they thought they were trying to pull, and he was grinning so much his mouth hurt.

When the food came they ate quickly because they were hungry. The boy couldn't finish his pie. He pushed what was left across the table and went to find the bathroom.

It was very fancy. When he backed away from the urinal it flushed all by itself because there was an electric eye built into the walls of the stall. It made him nervous to have stepped into the beam without realizing it, but when he found he could make the urinal flush over and over again by passing his hand in front of the beam, he felt better. It was watching him, but it wasn't very smart.

When he came out of the bathroom, he saw the

girl wasn't sitting at the table. She was standing by the cashier's counter. The old cleaning woman was holding her by the sweater and talking to the cashier. The girl kept shaking the fat hand away, but each time she did, the woman grabbed at her again.

Something had gone wrong.

The boy sidled over behind the rack of postcards. He began to study them intently. He was very still. He thought a person might walk right by and not see him.

The girl could see that the cashier didn't want trouble. She was young and pretty. She bit at her soft lower lip with tiny, perfect teeth. She kept fingering their key with her white fingers and trying to think while the old woman jabbered at her.

"There wasn't any luggage when I cleaned in there," said the old woman, pointing at the key. "That's why I checked back when I saw them leave. They spent the afternoon in the same bed. At her age." She looked at the girl, her tiny mouth puckered with satisfaction and disapproval. "I don't know what this world's coming to."

The girl felt her knees starting to shake. She didn't think she could stand what was going on in that woman's head. It was dirty and grubby in there, and she didn't want the old woman thinking about her.

"My dad is really going to be upset about this," she said as calmly as she could. She tried to get the cashier to look at her, but the young woman wouldn't do it.

"Where's your boyfriend?" demanded the cleaning lady, shaking her arm.

It was disgusting to be touched by her. There were patches of old-person sweat under the arms of her sleeveless dress.

"Don't touch me. My brother went back to our room. He's sick. When my dad gets . . ."

"Brother nothing. If you were my daughter I'd smack your bottom."

The woman had talked about her bottom. She had actually said the word. The girl felt so sick with rage and shame that she could hardly breathe. She suddenly wanted the boy very much, but she was afraid to look for him. It would be awful if they caught him, too.

"I think," said the cashier finally, "we'd better talk to Mr. Anderson about this." She looked at the girl for the first time. "I'm sorry," she added. "We have to be careful."

The girl didn't understand what she meant. What did they have to be careful about?

The cashier called over a waitress to take her place behind the counter. It was their waitress. Her eyes were big, and she wasn't smiling. The girl couldn't look at her. She let them lead her out of the silent restaurant. Someone scraped a knife against a plate.

Outside, she knew she should try to run. The cleaning lady was old and the cashier was wearing high heels. She could get away easily; but she couldn't run, she could barely walk. She had been caught, and she had never imagined what that would be like. Before, she had been happy. She had been crazy-happy, and had felt so light and airy that she had thought nothing could touch her. Now the old woman was pulling at her sweater and thinking bad thoughts about her. They clung like tar. She was wading through the dust of the parking lot, and it was so thick she could barely move.

Behind the desk in the motel lobby was a young man as neat and clean as a new piece of furniture. He seemed to have been waiting for them. He leaned forward politely. His eyes flickered.

"Some problem, Hazel?" he said to the cashier.

"You bet there is," said the old woman. She talked as if her words were punches, rocking back and forth, jabbing at the girl.

The girl tried to think of what she might say. She knew she wasn't going to give up. She wasn't going to be what the cleaning lady said she was. She would talk until they stopped believing her, and then she wouldn't say anything. She would never tell them her name. Her mother would never know. She couldn't let that happen.

"Miss Hendricks, is it?" said the man. He had flipped through a registration file and was holding up a white card. His face was carefully neutral. "Where are your parents now?"

"They're at the garage. Getting the car fixed. That's

where our luggage is, too. The car broke down when we were leaving this morning, that's why we didn't bring the luggage back. I thought my mom told you all about this."

The old woman with pink hair made a loud noise through her nose. The man coughed to cover the sound. He looked uncertainly, first at the girl and then at the cashier. The girl began to hope that he would believe her, at least for a while. She didn't know why it was important, but she wanted him to believe her.

"Well, that's right, I think. If you could just tell us the garage."

"I don't know the garage. Can't we just wait until my dad gets back? He's really going to be mad."

"I'm sorry, miss. Of course we can wait. Mrs. Purse just wants to be sure. Isn't that right, Mrs. Purse?" He looked at the old woman and she turned a mottled red. Even her fat upper arms.

"What about the boy?" she said, her voice tight. "I saw a boy, too, coming out of that room."

"Boy? What boy?" asked the man.

"My brother . . ." the girl began, but the man dropped the card on the desk as if he didn't want to touch it any longer.

"According to the registration there is a party of three in that room. Is that your mother and father and you?"

He looked at her very hard. Somewhere outside, a car alarm went off, but no one paid any attention.

They were all looking at her, and she didn't know what to say.

The old woman grabbed her arm again, triumphant. "There's just her and her boyfriend. There ain't any luggage. Just a paper bag with tampons in it." The woman made a disgusting noise with her mouth.

The girl thought she was going to cry. It was because the old woman had gone through her bag and found the tampons. She looked at the cashier, but the young woman looked ready to cry herself. That frightened her more than anything.

A second car alarm went off. In the motel lobby nothing moved but the man's eyes, darting from the old woman to the cashier, and finally to the girl.

He jumped when the fire alarm began to shriek. High and warbling, the sound was almost too loud to hear.

"Damn. Hazel? Check the parking lot. Keep her here, Mrs. Purse." He pointed a finger at the girl as he came out from behind the desk. "You're in trouble," he said.

A woman in a floral-print bathrobe came out into the lobby and tried to catch his arm as he brushed by.

"Is there a fire?" she asked.

"I'm checking," said the man, and disappeared through a large wooden door. The woman looked at the girl and the cleaning lady as if she was going to say something. She changed her mind and went back into her room.

Mrs. Purse hustled the girl over to a large leather

couch in front of the lobby window and pushed her down.

"You just sit there, missy," she said, standing over her, little fists on fat hips. "I have a granddaughter about your age. I don't know what I'd do if I thought she acted this way. I just don't know."

The girl wasn't listening. There was a very peculiar expression on her small narrow face. When Mrs. Purse recognized it, it took her breath away. The girl was trying not to smile. She was looking out through the lobby window and trying not to smile. Slowly the old woman turned.

He was staring through the darkening glass, watching her. His eyes were wide and dark, and with a tingle of outrage Mrs. Purse saw that his hair was entangled with green leaves and vines. As she watched, he leaned forward and pressed his hands and face against the glass so that his nose and lips were flattened.

The girl got up and calmly walked out the door. Outside, she turned and grinned with foxy eyes.

Mrs. Purse sat down on the couch with her hands on her chest and listened to the blood and the fire alarm pound in her ears.

"Wild things," she whispered. "Wicked wild things."

"Come on, you dope," said the girl. "You're going to give her a heart attack."

The boy smiled and climbed out of the laurel bushes planted in front of the window. They walked slowly through the crowd of motel guests waiting for something to happen in the parking lot. As they walked, the boy unwound the vine from around his head. No one tried to stop them.

The Highway

THE BOY woke up first, with a sore throat and dry, sticky eyelids. He sat very still, waiting until he was sure that he understood where they were.

It was the back seat of a car. Somebody's car. He didn't know whose. It was parked in a long driveway screened with dark evergreens. At the end of the driveway he could see the house of the people who owned the car. It had green shutters and a plastic deer in the front yard.

Beyond the house the sky was turning gray. They would have to move soon.

"Hey," he said softly.

She squirmed against him irritably and made a

small animal sound, clinging to sleep and dreams. There was no great hurry, he decided. She could finish the dream if she wanted to.

His nose was starting to run again. A clear, watery drip ran down over his upper lip. It was frustrating to have caught a cold.

He tipped his head back and tried to breathe gently through his mouth. The toilet paper she had given him back at the motel was gone. She had needed it herself during the night because they had left the paper bag in the motel room and the cleaning lady had found it.

He didn't want to think about the motel. He tilted his head to one side so he could see out across a grassy field to where the pine woods started. They looked so dark and deep. They looked as if they might go on forever. From the edge of the dinky little field to the end of the world.

There wasn't a bit of wind. Every blade of grass was perfectly still. He found he was holding his breath. Everything was so quiet and still that he didn't need to breathe.

He felt a deep longing swell inside his chest, almost lifting him from the seat. He wanted to get out of the car and walk into the woods. Walking away forever from camps, roads, motels, the sound of human voices. In that wood there were no paths, no clearings, no farm fences, no pylons stalking through the trees toward invisible cities. It would be safe there. They wouldn't be the same. They would be as light, as hard to detect, as shadows in shadows. They could simply disappear.

"What?" said the girl.

"Nothing," he said. "I must have been dreaming." He blinked and opened his eyes wide. There was a wind. It was moving the tops of the evergreens and shaking the television antenna on top of the house in a great invisible rush. Why had he thought there was no wind? He gave his head a shake, feeling its weight.

A light came on in the second story of the house. He could see a big shadow moving across the ceiling through the window.

"Hey," he said again. "The people in the house are waking up."

The girl wiped her face against his sleeve and sat up. "Yuck," she said. "This blanket is all dog hair."

They hadn't noticed in the dark when they had found the car unlocked. The blanket that had been folded on the back seat was covered with soft yellow hair.

"Well, it doesn't matter now."

"Yeah, but I'm going to take about a million baths when we get home."

He tried to think what that would be like. Would he be sitting in some strange apartment that afternoon, trying to talk to her mother while she took a bath? It didn't seem very likely somehow.

She stiffened slightly and began to explore under the blanket with her hand. He understood that she was feeling inside her pants, and he closed his eyes to give her some privacy. He was beginning to feel defeated. He couldn't understand why. They didn't have to take any more chances. Perhaps it was his cold, and this other thing that she had, that made everything so complicated. It didn't seem as if anything was going to work.

"I've got to find a bathroom soon," she said in a small, flat voice.

Through the windshield he saw a woman with her hair in curlers open the door of the house. A big golden dog pushed by her and bounded stiff-legged out into the wet grass. It rushed the plastic deer and sniffed suspiciously.

The woman went back in the house.

"Oh no," said the girl. The dog was running down the drive sideways toward the car. "Do you think it knows we're here?"

"It doesn't make any difference," he said, pushing the blanket aside and fumbling for the door handle.

"But what if it bites?"

"It's a golden retriever. They don't bite people." He wasn't really sure about that, but he was willing to take the chance. He didn't want the people to find them in their car. He didn't think he could stand people anymore.

When he pushed the door open he almost hit the dog. It shied off the driveway in astonishment, scattering gravel with its big feet.

The boy got out of the car slowly. "Hi, dog," he

said, holding out the back of his hand so the dog could sniff at him. He could see it was confused. Its hackles were up, but it was wagging its tail.

Out of the corner of his eye he saw that the girl was out of the car and moving flat-footed toward the road.

"Don't run," he said. She had left the door open, so he took a step back and slammed it closed.

The dog was offended. It barked once, loudly, and then made a grab at his ankles. He decided that it might be better to run, after all. It was hard going, because the dog was knocking against him. It wasn't vicious, but it kept trying to eat his sneakers.

When he reached the road he stopped and pointed back down the drive. "Go home!" he said. The dog sat down and grinned at him.

"I thought you said not to run," said the girl.

"What do you mean? He was chewing on me!"

Her hair and shirt were wet and covered with white flecks. When he looked closely he saw that they were flowers. Her hair was filled with tiny white blossoms.

"What happened to you?"

"I ran into a bush."

"See. I told you not to run."

He suddenly felt lighthearted again. The dog hadn't really hurt him, and maybe her mother would let them stay together, after all. It was possible. He reached out and began to pluck the blossoms from her dark head one by one.

"You look like Spring," he said.

"What do you mean, spring?" she asked. She was suspicious, but she tipped her head down so he could get the flowers out of her hair.

"No, I mean it. It's this lady in a painting. She's Spring." He had had sort of a crush on the lady in the painting, actually. She didn't in fact look like the girl, but their smiles were the same.

"Is she pretty?" asked the girl. She knew she was asking for it, but she felt brave.

"Of course. She has flowers in her hair. Just like you." The flowers were wet and sticky and clung to his fingers. "You can see right through her clothes."

She shoved him hard, and he almost fell over the dog. It started barking as loudly as it could, and they took off running, hardly caring where they were going.

The sun was already hot on the backs of their necks when they found a gas station that was open.

A teenager with bad acne and long black hair was wheeling a Pennzoil sign out of the garage. He positioned it carefully in front of the pumps and watched the girl go around to the ladies' room at the side of the station. He looked at the boy and then went back into the garage.

"It's locked," said the girl, coming back.

"Can you wait?"

She shook her head.

"Well, we'll get the key."

They walked together into the office. Through the door into the garage they could see the teenager pushing a large red jack under a pickup.

The key was hanging on one end of the counter. It was attached to a chunk of broom handle. Someone had written WOMAN on the broom handle with a Magic Marker.

The girl started to lift it off the hook.

"Hey!" yelled the teenager. He dropped the jack handle and came into the office.

"That's for customers," he said, putting out his hand to stop the key from swinging on its hook. He lounged against the counter, smiling and nodding, as if he had just made a very clever move and wanted to see what they would do next.

"Can I have a Mars bar, please?" said the boy.

The teenager looked puzzled, but he unlocked the counter with a key attached to his belt by a long, heavy chain.

"Thirty-five cents," he said, keeping his hand on the candy bar.

The girl counted the money carefully out of the palm of her hand onto the counter.

"Can we have the key, please?" said the boy.

"I said that was for customers."

The boy looked at the money.

"Damn," said the teenager, but he gave the girl the key.

"You wait outside," he said to the boy when she was gone. He had stopped smiling.

"Okay. Is this the way to Ahlburg?"

"Yeah." The teenager looked curious for the first time. "You walking to Ahlburg? That's ten miles."

"No. I just wanted to know."

The teenager nodded, not believing him, so the boy went outside and stood by the Pennzoil sign.

When the boy and girl were gone, the teenager went into the office to see if she had put the key back. Satisfied, he followed them out to the edge of the highway. He could see them walking toward Ahlburg. That's what they were doing. They had unwrapped the candy bar and were sharing it.

A battered Jeepster pulled up by the pumps behind him. On the door was a faded sign that said HOF-STADDER'S GOAT FARM. He looked at the Jeepster, and then at the two kids. He thought a minute, and then started walking toward the Jeepster. The more he thought, the faster he walked. He had started to grin again.

"Ten miles," the girl was saying. "I thought it was supposed to be eight."

"I think this guy probably didn't know. He didn't seem too smart." The boy had to clear his throat to talk. The Mars bar had made him thirsty.

"Yeah. Still. Do you think we should try to hitch?"

"I thought you weren't supposed to."

"No. But maybe we should." She was a little worried about him. She could hear him breathing. He made little whistling sounds. She wasn't sure, but she didn't think when you had a cold you were supposed to make little whistling sounds.

The boy shook his head. He didn't feel that great, but he didn't want to talk to people. It made him tired. Tireder than walking. He wished they could leave the highway and walk through the woods. It looked cool up there in the trees, and the road was so hot. If he could get away from the highway, he was sure he'd feel better.

When he looked ahead he could see that a Jeepster had pulled onto the shoulder in front of them with its motor running. The back of the truck was coated with dust, but he could see the shadow of a man's head, cocked to watch them in the rearview mirror.

They tried to go around the Jeepster. It smelled of dust, hot oil, and burning gas.

As they came up on the passenger side, the man stuck his arm out and worked the handle on the outside of the door. The door swung open in front of them. They would have to go down in the ditch to get around. The ditch was filled with tall wet grass and weeds. The boy looked at the man.

"Hi there! You need a lift to Ahlburg? Hop in." The man had ginger hair and sore blue eyes.

"No thanks," said the boy, and tried to nudge the girl into the ditch.

"Hey," she said, grabbing his arm so she wouldn't fall.

"Hold on. Don't be in such a hurry," said the man. He reached into the breast pocket of his flannel shirt and pulled out a wallet. When he flipped it open, the boy could see a large golden badge. He had to hold on to the truck door to keep from slipping.

"See that?" said the man. "That means I'm a deputy sheriff. You've got nothing to be afraid of. Come on. Hop in. Ahlburg is too far to walk."

The boy looked at the girl. He could tell she wanted to take the ride. Ten miles wasn't far. Maybe it would all be over in a few minutes.

The front seat of the Jeepster was slick yellow plastic. When the girl was inside, the man reached across them both and pulled the door shut. The handle on the inside was missing. That bothered the boy. Someone had once told him that you should never get in a car with a missing door handle if you're hitchhiking. He didn't know why exactly. It hadn't seemed to matter because he never hitched rides. Now it was too late to figure it out. The Jeepster was already moving fast down the highway.

The man fumbled with his right hand in a pack of cigarettes on the dusty dashboard.

"Smoke?" he asked, lighting up. He did it in a showy way, manipulating a book of matches with one hand.

The boy shook his head. It surprised him that the man should think he might want a cigarette. He wondered how old he thought they were.

"Name's Hofstadder. Pearly Hofstadder. You're?" He leaned forward over the steering wheel, looking first at the girl and then at the boy.

"Howie," said the boy under his breath. He didn't

really want the man to hear. He felt miserable. The inside of the Jeep was hot, and there was a bad smell. He thought it was the man who smelled, even though he looked clean.

Hofstadder must have known what he was thinking, because he said suddenly, "Sorry about the smell, Howie."

It made the boy jump. The man had got his name. Right off.

"It's goats. Had to carry one of my bucks in the back a week ago. Still stinks. Ain't nothing that smells worse than a goat. Ain't that right, Howie?"

The boy nodded, but he couldn't get it out of his head that it was really Hofstadder who smelled. The man kept looking at the girl out of the pink corners of his eyes.

After about two miles the Jeepster turned abruptly off the highway onto a dirt road.

"Hey," said the boy. "Isn't Ahlburg that way? We'd better get off here."

"You in some kind of hurry? I just have to pick up some stuff at the house. Won't take a minute." The Jeepster didn't slow down. They could hear the tires drumming over the ruts and the stones kicked up inside the fenders. The trees on either side of the road were coated with fine yellow dust.

"You the kids who jumped camp the other day?" said the man. He nodded when they didn't answer. "I thought it might be you. What have you been doing? How'd you get over to Barnesville?"

"We got a ride. We're going back now. They know we're coming. They're waiting for us."

"Sure. But what you been doing?" The man smiled. He had a big mouth, and when he smiled the boy could see he didn't have any teeth except in front. "Getting a little nudgy, uh?"

"What do you mean?"

"You know what I mean, Howie. Hell, I don't mind. I'm a liberal. It's okay by me if you kids have a little fun. I'll bet you and your girl have had a high old time. Ain't that right, Howie?"

"It's none of your business," whispered the girl.

"What's that?" said the man sharply.

The boy sat up quickly. "I think we should get out here," he said. "We can walk. We don't mind."

The man pressed him back in the seat with a huge forearm. It felt like wood. "Cool it, hotshot. You're not going anywhere." He gripped the steering wheel with both hands and stared grimly out of the dirty windshield. "You might even say you're under arrest."

"What do you mean, arrest?"

The man didn't answer. He pulled the truck off the road in front of a store.

There were no other buildings nearby, and the store was empty, abandoned. The windows were smashed and the steps burned away. There was a dilapidated phone booth at one end.

The man turned off the ignition and looked at them. He wasn't pretending to be friendly anymore.

"You're the ones who set off the fire alarm at the

Starlight last night, ain't you? You know that's a serious offense? You need all the friends you can get. You and Jailbait, there." He spat out the window. "I'm going to call the sheriff now. You just sit tight, you hear?"

The man rolled up both windows, first the one by the girl and then the one on the driver's side. The heat and stench of goat were terrible. He nodded at them slowly, as if he had done something clever, and then got out of the truck. He slammed the door behind him. As he walked toward the phone booth he watched them over his shoulder. He looked smug, almost happy. Pardoe and the cleaning lady had looked smug, too. The man was so sure, so very sure that there was nothing they could do.

"What's going to happen?" She could barely talk. "Do you think they'll put us in jail?"

"I don't know. I don't even think this guy is a real sheriff. He doesn't act right."

"Oh God, he's so weird. Where is he taking us? Do you think we should try to run?"

"I don't know," said the boy, but he understood now why the man had rolled up the windows. The inside handles on both doors had been removed. "We're locked in. We'd have to roll down the windows and crawl out. I don't think we could make it."

The man was watching them from the phone booth, even as he dialed. It was as if he was daring them.

"What do you think? Do you think we could make it?"

She didn't answer. When he tore his eyes away from the man in the phone booth, he saw she was staring at a gold charm in the shape of a goat's head. It was turning slowly in the still air. It was hanging from a key, and the key was in the truck's ignition.

The Woods

MADDY HAD forgotten that it was Parents' Day, or perhaps she had never understood what that meant. The camp parking lot was filling up with cars. Parents and grandparents picked their way slowly forward, smiling up at the roofs of the camp buildings which poked above the trees. They carried shopping bags of Fritos, Ding Dongs, Twinkies, special longed-for boxes of crackers, and cheese spread in aerosol containers.

At the foot of the macadam path leading up to the camp, a folding table had been set up. Over it was a yellow umbrella strung with pinecones and paper chains. Girls with calm, self-conscious faces were distributing name tags and directions. The name tags were in the shape of large yellow daisies. They stuck to anything. Tweed and linen jackets, silk blouses and T-shirts.

No one offered Maddy a name tag. She didn't belong there, and she couldn't find a place to stand up or sit down.

Margo Cutter brought her a cup of lemonade and then wandered back to stand with her friends near the reception table. Occasionally one of the young women would glance at Maddy. If Maddy caught her eye, the woman's face would immediately assume an expression of sincere concern.

To escape, Maddy picked her way among the parked cars to the entrance of the parking lot.

She noticed that she still had the cup of lemonade in her hand. It felt sticky. She set it carefully upright on a wooden post as a patrol car stopped near her and a short stocky woman got out. Maddy watched her. She felt suddenly very alert. Her fingertips tingled.

"Mrs. Golden? I'm Sarah Gallagher. County juvenile officer?"

Maddy nodded. She was the woman who didn't know anything.

"I'm afraid we have a problem, Mrs. Golden."

"What's wrong?"

"Your daughter and the boy were picked up this morning near Barnesville. By one of Sheriff Prosser's deputies."

Maddy looked over the woman's shoulder at the patrol car. It was empty.

"Where are they?" she asked.

"Well, we don't know, exactly. I'm afraid they stole his truck, Mrs. Golden."

Maddy waited. There was more coming. She could tell.

"They didn't go far. Just down the road. The deputy wasn't able to follow them from there. I'm afraid they ran over his foot, Mrs. Golden."

Margo appeared at Maddy's side, hovering uncertainly. "What's wrong?" she asked.

"Laura's run over a policeman's foot," Maddy said. "Oh, my God!"

"Don't be too upset, now," said Miss Gallagher. She spoke to Margo, who seemed to be reacting in the right way. "The deputy wasn't badly hurt. Just some bruises. And while I can't promise anything, I don't think Sheriff Prosser is going to make any charges here. He thinks the deputy mishandled the business. He turned off the highway to find a phone booth, and left the kids alone in the truck with the key in the ignition. He wasn't in uniform. Sheriff Prosser thinks that Laura and Howie must have been frightened in some way. These aren't the caliber of kids we normally deal with."

Margo shook her head rapidly. No. No, they weren't that caliber of kids. Over her shoulder Maddy watched a tall young girl come out into the parking lot and be enthusiastically embraced by an older couple. Maddy wondered who she was, and if Laura had once counted her as a friend.

"What did he do?"

Miss Gallagher didn't understand.

"The deputy," Maddy explained. "He must have done something. They wanted to come here. To me. And he didn't let them." She put her hand to her temple. The sun was beginning to make her head ache. "Why are we driving them away? I don't understand that. Why are we driving them away?"

Miss Gallagher looked at Margo and then at Maddy. "Mrs. Golden, I think it would be best if I drove you back to your motel now. I'm sure that they'll be picked up before long."

"You don't think she'll come here?"

Miss Gallagher looked uncomfortable. "Barnesville is nearly ten miles away, Mrs. Golden. Perhaps it would be better if we waited at the motel. Margo will stay here. In case they show up." Maddy looked at the two of them. They were both nodding their heads at her in the same encouraging way. Miss Gallagher had called Margo by her name. Maddy hadn't realized that they knew each other. It was not unreasonable, perhaps, but she hadn't known. She wondered how much else she didn't know.

Back in the motel room Maddy took off her shoes and lay down on the bed. She had lost track of Miss Gallagher, but she assumed she was somewhere in the room, waiting. She apparently didn't need to talk. That was a relief. Maddy wanted to study the ceiling, where light reflected from the motel pool wavered through a succession of bright patterns. It was like a dance of light and shadow, of coming together and parting.

She began to wonder if she would ever find her way to Laura. Somehow, in a way she didn't understand, the chance seemed to be slipping away, lost in misunderstandings and casually inflicted hurts.

The boy leaned over the railing of the bridge and peered down at the river. It was stained brown with mud, its surface marked with long smooth ripples and broad undulations. He could see the reflection of his head, a dark knob on the reflection of the bridge itself. He leaned out farther, testing for the point of balance where his feet might lift from the pavement.

"Hey! Are you watching?" called the girl, sticking her head out of the phone booth.

"Yes." He pushed away from the railing and looked up and down the highway. "I'm watching."

The road cut straight through the pine forest, and from the bridge he could see for miles. There were no cars, not even a house or a barn in the distance. The old man who had lent them change for the telephone was sitting by a small white shed just where the road rose to cross the river. His name was Mr. Lockwood, and he sold honey. He couldn't have sold much, there was so little traffic. Perhaps he didn't mind. He had pulled a wooden kitchen chair into a patch of sun. He sat up very straight, but so still he might have been asleep.

The girl was talking to someone now. Behind the dusty glass of the booth she had taken out the little

notebook and was writing somethin
couldn't hear what she was saying.

He wondered what had happened to
the Jeepster. He hadn't been badly hurt whe
had sideswiped him. He had gotten up rig
The boy had watched him in the rearview
Perhaps the man wasn't looking for them, afte
Maybe he was embarrassed because he had tried
lock them in the Jeepster. As the boy considered this
possibility it seemed less and less likely. No, the man
was out there somewhere, trying to figure out where
they were.

The girl hung up the phone and squeezed out of the
booth, fighting for a moment with the stubborn door.

"Did you talk to her?" he asked. "Was your mom
there?"

She shook her head. Her face was pale. She seemed
dazed by what she had heard.

"What's wrong? Didn't she come?"

"She's there. But not at the camp. At a motel. In
Ahlburg."

"A motel?" He didn't understand.

"She's been there since the day before yesterday.
Mr. Wells called her when we didn't go back to camp.
She drove up right away. Miss Haskell said she was
sick with worry." The girl put her fingertips to her lips
and stared at nothing. "Oh God. She's going to be so
mad at me. Why didn't we think that Mr. Wells would
call her? Why didn't we think?"

g down. The boy
down. the man with
he man the truck
en the truck away.
ght away. mirror.
mirror. all.
all. to

obvious now that her
happened and come
was supposed to do,
lly care. It was un-
't help it.
l today," he said
you talked to her."
nom him wildly. "She didn't
t you see? She didn't understand!"

...ached out and touched her shoulder, but she
...ook his hand away. He felt slow and dumb, like a
windup toy beginning to run down.

"Do my mom and dad know? Did Miss Haskell say?"

"Mr. Wells sent a telegram. They haven't heard anything yet." She spoke over her shoulder, her voice soft
and tired. "She said you can't come home with me and
Mom. It's illegal or something. You have to stay at
camp until they hear from your parents."

He wasn't surprised. He had always known, really,
that there would be some rule like that.

"We won't get to visit the sliced-up people," he said
sadly, but she wasn't listening.

"Do you think Mom knows about that man? About
how we took his truck?"

"I don't know. Maybe not yet."

"What am I going to tell her? She's going to kill me."

"No, she won't. I won't let her." That was a joke, of
course. He wished it wasn't, but that's all it was. Her
mother would decide what she wanted, and there

wasn't much he could do about it. Still, he had made the girl smile. When she turned and looked at him, he saw that she was smiling and crying at the same time. She could cry like nobody's business. There were even tears on her glasses.

"Here," he said, taking them off her face and wiping them on his shirttail.

"I've got to call Mom now," she said as she watched. "Miss Haskell gave me the number. We'll borrow some more money from Mr. Lockwood. Do you think he'll mind?"

"No. He's nice. We can give him an IOU."

"I'll tell her that we *have* to stay together. If she can't take us both, I'll stay at camp. We'll run away again if we have to. Really."

"Yes," he said, but he couldn't meet her eyes. He was ashamed because he didn't believe her. Should he tell her that he wanted to run away right now? Would she be willing to disappear into the woods with him? He almost smiled. How crazy that idea was. Just a stupid dream. He would never tell her. There would never be a time. She would go back to the city with her mother and he would stay at camp and be a goat. That was what everyone would want. That was the rule. He shivered and looked up where the sun was blazing in the pale dome of the sky. Maybe he should be a bandit like Calvin had said and make his own rules.

She ran ahead of him to Mr. Lockwood's stand. When he joined her she had more change in her hand,

and the old man was carefully studying the note she had written. He folded it neatly and put it in his pocket.

"I'm going to call now," she said. "Are you coming?"

"No. I'll wait here."

The old man smiled at him when she was gone.

"You look right beat," he said, and offered the boy a Mason jar filled with bright red Kool-Aid. It was warm and sweet, with a faint musty aftertaste.

"I make that with honey," said the old man. "Keeps me traveling. You a traveling man?"

The boy shook his head. Goat, bandit, traveling man. He didn't know.

"I thought maybe you were a traveling man. Come far?"

The boy shrugged, not knowing how to measure the distance, but he tried to smile.

"Far to go?"

Behind the honey stand a narrow trail ran back into the woods. It was overgrown with shrubs and dry grass. It didn't look as if many people ever went that way.

"No. Not far."

The phone rang. Once, then twice. Maddy heard a chair creak as Miss Gallagher stirred impatiently. Very slowly, her body as fragile as ash, Maddy sat up and picked up the phone.

"Mom?"

Maddy began to cry. "Oh, Laura darling . . ."

"There was this man," Laura said slowly, as if she were going to tell Maddy a long and intricate story. "He said he was a deputy . . ."

"Yes, I know. He didn't hurt you, did he?"

"No. He was acting so strange . . . We hit him with a truck, Mom. It was an accident."

"Yes, I know, darling. It's all right. He wasn't hurt. He won't bother you anymore, I promise. Don't be afraid."

"We're not afraid. We're not afraid anymore." The connection was poor. Laura's voice was faint, vibrating against the hum of a thousand other conversations.

"Mom? I got your number from Miss Haskell at camp."

"Yes, that was the right thing to do. I'm so glad you thought of that. But where are you, Laura? Please tell me."

"Miss Haskell said that Howie has to stay at camp. That he can't come home with me."

"That's not true, darling. She doesn't know. He is coming. I promise."

"We've got to stay together, Mom." Laura's voice was thin and stretched.

"I promise, I promise. He is coming home with us. I'll steal him, anything. Just tell me where you are. I want you so much."

There was a long pause. Maddy felt afraid. She tried to stop crying so she could hear.

"I don't know, Mom. Don't cry." Her voice faded and grew strong again, as if she had looked away from the telephone. "It's pretty here. There're trees, and a river. There's an old man, too. He lent us some money so I could call you."

"But . . ." Maddy tried to think. "Is it a pay phone? What's the number? It should be right there. Right where you dial."

"There isn't one. Somebody scratched it off." Laura's voice suddenly sounded very tired. As if things had become too hard. Too hard to try anymore.

"I'm sorry that things didn't work out at camp, Mom. I really tried."

"That doesn't matter, darling. Not anymore. Just stay where you are. Promise me that, Laura. I'll find you. Just stay where you are."

There was a series of sharp clicks, and a woman's voice, clear and impersonal, said, "Please deposit five cents. Five cents. Please deposit five cents."

"Mom?" Maddy heard Laura say, and then there was nothing at all.

Miss Gallagher took the phone from her hand. "Dial 911, Laura," she said confidently into the dead receiver. "Dial 911." The silence was replaced by a dial tone.

Miss Gallagher listened for a moment, her eyes staring into Maddy's. She hung up the phone. "Where is she, Mrs. Golden? What did she say?"

Maddy could hardly see her. The world seemed to be drowning in a pool of her own tears.

"She didn't know. There was a river. Trees." What

did it mean? It was a state full of rivers and trees, going on forever.

"A pay phone. Don't forget that." Miss Gallagher looked thoughtful. She opened her white wicker handbag and took out a map. She unfolded it and spread it on the bed. Here, she explained, is where the truck was found. They couldn't have gone too far on foot. This must be the river that Laura mentioned. As her blunt finger rooted through the tangle of red-and-blue lines, Maddy began to feel some hope.

"She said there was an old man. He lent her some money." How foolish that sounded. Old men weren't fixtures. They weren't marked on maps.

Miss Gallagher nodded. "Lockwood. He's got a honey stand by the bridge on County M. There's a pay phone there, too."

She folded up the map in the right way, so that it fell obediently along its original creases. Maddy began to respect Miss Gallagher. She knew how to fold a map. Perhaps she knew where Laura was.

"This is the place," said Miss Gallagher. Maddy looked out the car window at the river, the trees, an enormous sky hazy with a long afternoon's heat. There was a small stand by the bridge. It was painted a glistening white. One corner was sinking into a clump of goldenrod. A hand-painted sign said LOCKWOOD'S HONEY.

There was no one there. Large plywood shutters

closed off the interior of the stand as firmly as eyelids seal the eyes.

Maddy got out of the car. Her legs were a little shaky. She was used to seeing countryside through the closed windows of a swiftly moving vehicle. It made her feel vulnerable and slow to be standing there by the side of the road. She could feel the coarse gravel through the thin soles of her shoes and the wind moving against her bare arms. She could smell the pine trees. She had forgotten that pine trees had such a rich, promising smell. She thought Laura must be very brave to have come here, to be willing to stay, even until dark.

An old man came out of the woods behind the honey stand. He was wearing a black suit and a very white shirt, and he moved with a spry limp.

"I'll just open up," he said. He picked up a long prop of peeled white wood and lifted one of the shutters. Behind it Maddy could see shelves lined with greenish-gold jars of honey.

Miss Gallagher came around from her side of the car. "Mr. Lockwood? Have you seen a young girl and boy here? About half an hour ago. They might have used the pay phone."

The man paused, bending for the second prop. He was very old, with black liquid eyes in a dry face.

"Oh yes. I seen them." He calculated, putting out a pale tongue. "Are you going to pay me?" he asked abruptly.

"What do you mean, pay you?" Miss Gallagher was indignant.

The man chuckled and straightened up. As he came close to them, he extracted a folded piece of paper from the breast pocket of his jacket. It had been torn from a small spiral notebook. He smoothed it carefully with his fingers and then put it in Maddy's hand.

"IOU," it said. "Sixty cents. Shadow Golden."

"Yes, of course I'll pay you. I'm her mother." Maddy fumbled for her purse.

"Shadow's mother?" The old man recaptured the slip of paper neatly from Maddy's hand.

"Don't have to pay. You'd want the IOU then, wouldn't you? I'd rather have the IOU."

He folded the small page up carefully and put it away. Maddy could hardly bear it.

"But where are they? Where did they go?"

The old man turned and looked off into the woods and then up at the sun, trying to get his bearings.

"That way," he said, waving his hand toward a dirt track that followed the bank of the river away from the highway.

"That road? But where does it go?"

"Not a road. Fire trail. Doesn't go anywhere. Just up in the woods. I told them, but they seemed to know what they were doing. Sweet kids. Do you want some honey?"

Maddy shook her head, and the old man snatched

away the white wooden prop. The shutter fell down with a bang.

"Up in the woods, it goes. That's where they are now."

Overhead a helicopter was circling. As it passed low above them it made a terrific racket, its blades chopping frantically as if they meant to destroy the air itself. From their hiding place underneath an old spruce, the girl and boy watched it suddenly rise vertically into the air and sweep off to the west.

"Do you think they're looking for us?" she asked.

"No. Why would they be looking for us?"

The girl thought there might be reasons. They had done all those things. Sneaking into that motel. Stealing. They'd taken that man's truck. They hadn't taken it very far, but still they'd taken it, and they hadn't asked. Would that be enough for them to send out helicopters? Were men with guns looking for them? She didn't know. It seemed possible.

"Well, I don't think they saw us. I mean, if they are looking for us. Do you?"

The boy didn't answer. She wished he would say something. When she had told him what her mother had said, he had simply nodded and walked off along the fire trail. She didn't know where they were going, or what he was thinking.

It upset her that he wouldn't talk. There were things she wanted them to think about together. She wanted to tell him that her mother had cried on the telephone. She hadn't expected that. She had thought her mother would be mad. Trying not to show it, perhaps, but still mad underneath. Her mother wasn't mad. She was afraid. It made the girl afraid, too.

It frightened her to realize how much she mattered to her mother. She knew her mother loved her. She'd always known that. But she had always believed that her mother was safe. Safe from her. That she didn't have to think about Maddy when she did something. But that wasn't right. She had to think. She had to think because she had made her mother listen.

When she was little and her mother wouldn't listen, she would punch her. She would punch her as hard as she could. Sometimes her mother had laughed, and sometimes she had been angry, but she had never cried. When the girl had been little she hadn't been able to hurt anyone. Now she could.

The funny thing was that, in some queer, nervous way, she felt glad. She felt very real, as if her body had suddenly gained an enormous presence and weight. She wanted to talk about that, too.

She looked at the boy. The helicopter was gone, but he showed no inclination to move. He was sitting with his legs drawn up, one cheek resting on his knee, his arms tucked away across his chest. His eyes were open, but she couldn't tell what he was thinking. It made her sad that she couldn't tell what he was thinking.

"Where are we going?"

"I don't know. Somewhere." It was as if he couldn't bring himself to tell her.

"Mom said we should wait for her at the bridge. She said she'd find us." She had already told him that. "She said Miss Haskell was wrong. That you could come home with us. She promised."

He took a deep breath and straightened up, as if he had finally decided to talk. "No, she didn't."

"What do you mean? Yes, she did!"

"No, she didn't. She couldn't. Miss Haskell is right." He stood up and turned away so she couldn't see his face. "It's against the law."

"What is?"

"I don't know. Us."

"That's crazy," she said. She was angry now. At him. Because he was making her afraid. "That's crazy. You're crazy."

He didn't answer, but he looked at her. He was holding his head up, and his eyes were narrow. It was as if he wanted to show her that he wasn't crying. But he was, almost.

"I think we should go back," she said. "I mean, maybe you can't come home with me right away. Then I'll stay at camp. But I think we should go back. There's no place else to go."

"Yes, there is. I'm not going back there. Not ever. You go. I didn't say you had to come."

She couldn't breathe. She was ready to cry herself.

With anger, terror, she didn't know. "I thought we were supposed to stay together."

"No, we aren't. They won't let us." He tried to think of something to say that would make her feel everything he was afraid of. "I don't need you. I don't want you anymore."

They stared at each other over a wilderness that words had made, and then she jumped him, wrestling him to the ground and pounding at his face with her fists. He felt his glasses snap at the bridge, and relief swept over him like a wave. He was almost choking with it. He had never felt so strong in his life. He caught her hands, and twisted, forcing her over on her back so he could sit on her stomach. She didn't give up. She didn't seem to realize she was losing.

"You take that back, you bastard!" she panted. "You take that back!"

"I take it back. I didn't mean it. You know I didn't mean it."

She stopped fighting then. It was funny. He was sitting on top of her, holding her hands back over her head, but she had won.

"I didn't mean it," he said again. She tried to smile, but had to sniff instead. Her face was wet, and her nose was running. He thought she looked beautiful.

"I know. But you still can't say that."

He let her go, and she sat up. They sat crosslegged, close together, their heads touching. For the moment they weren't able to look at each other, but they fumbled with each other's hands.

"I'm sorry I broke your glasses."

"Yeah. That's okay."

"Can you see all right?"

"Yes. No, not really. Everything's fuzzy."

"You can wear mine. We can take turns or something."

He smiled when he thought of that.

"No, it's okay. I've got some spare ones. Back at camp. Okay?"

He felt her head nod against his.

"Okay," she whispered. He caught her nervous hand and held it. She gave it up to him like a gift. It wasn't very clean. There was dirt under her nails, and there was a shiny callus on her second finger where she would hold a pencil. He was surprised again at how long her fingers were. They looked delicate, almost fragile, but he knew they weren't.

"Listen," he said. "There's something I wanted to tell you about."

"What?"

"Well, it's kind of weird. I had this idea. About us. I had this idea that just you and me could live together in the woods. Sort of like Indians. We could get what we needed from, I don't know, fields and cottages, and no one would ever see us or bother us again. They wouldn't be able to, because we wouldn't ever be there when they looked for us." He knew he wasn't being very clear, that she wouldn't be able to feel the magic of the idea, but that wasn't important, really. He didn't have to persuade her. He could let it go now.

"I used to think about it a lot, and sometimes I wanted to tell you, but I was afraid you would think it was just crazy." He tried to laugh, but kept his head down in case she should want to look at his face. "It is crazy, isn't it?"

"Yeah. Kind of. It's nice to think about, though. We could build a raft and go down the river. Just floating along." She sniffed and laughed at the same time. "I'd have to learn how to swim. Finally." Her head knocked against his as she thought. "The trouble is, we couldn't go to Greece. I really want to do that when we're older, don't you?"

"Yes. We will, too."

"And what if one of us got sick?"

"I don't know." He was genuinely surprised. "I never thought about that."

"Well. We would think of something. We always do."

Suddenly he was very sure that everything was going to be all right. He wasn't a fool. He knew that there would be arguments and long-distance phone calls, and parents and camp counselors and policemen talking over their heads about things he didn't understand. He would want to crawl in a hole, and she would cry. It didn't matter. They would think of something.

They could look at each other now and smile.

"We better get going," he said. "Your mom's going to be worried."

"That's okay." Some of her toughness had come back. "She'll get over it."

They climbed down to the path together and started back along the fire trail toward the bridge. The sun was shining. They could feel its warmth in their hair and on their faces. Small birds darted ahead of them, ducking and weaving, leading the way through the pines and the dry summer grass.

"There's Mom," said the girl.

Howie looked up. The woman was just a blur, coming fast. When she was close enough, he would see her face. He wondered what he would find there.

A stump loomed in front of them, splitting the path. They drifted apart, their clasped hands rising as it came between them.

"Hold on," Laura said. "Hold on."